A KIND OF TESTAMENT
WITOLD GOMBROWICZ

EDITED BY DOMINIQUE DE ROUX
TRANSLATED BY ALASTAIR HAMILTON

WITH AN INTRODUCTION BY
MAURICE NADEAU

Dalkey Archive Press
Champaign • London

Originally published in French as *Entretiens de Dominique de Roux avec Gombrowicz* by Editions Pierre Belfond, 1968.

First published in Great Britain in 1973 by Calder & Boyars, Ltd.

Published by arrangement with Marion Boyars Publishers

Library of Congress Cataloging-in-Publication Data

Gombrowicz, Witold.
 [Entretiens avec Gombrowicz. English]
 A kind of testament / Witold Gombrowicz ; edited by Dominique de
Roux ; translated by Alastair Hamilton ; with an introduction by
Maurice Nadeau. -- 1st paperback ed.
    p. cm.
 Translation of Gombrowicz's answers to questions asked by Dominique
de Roux, contained in Entretiens avec Gombrowicz.
 Originally published: London : Calder and Boyars, 1973.
 Includes bibliographical references.
 ISBN-13: 978-1-56478-476-6 (alk. paper)
 ISBN-10: 1-56478-476-2 (alk. paper)
 1. Gombrowicz, Witold--Interviews. 2. Authors, Polish--20th
century--Interviews. I. Roux, Dominique de. II. Title.
 PG7158.G6692A3513 2007
 891.8'5373--dc22
 [B]

2007026693

Partially funded by a grant from the Illinois Arts Council, a state Agency, and by the University of Illinois, Urbana-Champaign.

Dalkey Archive Press is a nonprofit organization whose mission is to promote international cultural understanding and provide a forum for dialogue for the literary arts.

www.dalkeyarchive.com

Printed on permanent/durable acid-free paper and bound in the United States of America.

CONTENTS

INTRODUCTION

Maurice Nadeau

Witold Gombrowicz was fifty-four years old when, with the translation of *Ferdydurke* into French, he acquired an international reputation. His genius was acknowledged late, even though his literary career had started early. Permanently dissatisfied (although he subsequently won the International Publishers' Prize and his plays enjoyed a certain success) as well as being seriously ill, Gombrowicz was all the more eager to make himself known and to reveal the 'secrets' of a work which he considered to have been largely misunderstood. After writing this 'kind of testament' he only had a few months left to live.

His aim was to intrigue the reader, to surprise and to astonish him—and it must be admitted that he succeeded. The 'testament' is astonishing not so much because of its 'revelations', which are deliberately paradoxical or even provocative, as because of the immutable self-confidence which Gombrowicz managed to sustain in the worst situations of his life (a twenty-three year exile in a continent where, to begin with, he could not even speak the language) and because of the equally unshakeable confidence he had in his work. He knew it was new, original, imperishable. He was a part of it. It expressed, as he wrote, his most intimate, most unadulterated and indomitable self in his long struggle with an arduous existence—a struggle to conquer a 'form' of his own. His work was his victory and he was justly proud of it.

Yet he regarded this victory as dubious to the extent in which his work existed independently, detached itself from its author and, like every living organism, possessed a structure and a 'form' which guaranteed its perenniality. But wasn't Gombrowicz's struggle, through which he endeavoured to define himself, directed against 'form', that anticipation of death? And did he not finally take possession of it in order to become a writer, an artist? He, more than anyone else, enclosed himself in the dilemma that literature has been trying to solve since time immemorial. His genius consists in having turned this paradox into the very matter of his work, in having given 'formlessness' such a 'form' that the discussion always remains open onto a reality which rises above it on all sides. Yet, at the same time, the discussion is undermined by putting itself into question, for, in his own peculiar way, Gombrowicz insinuated himself into the heart of the work of art in order to blow it up. He destroyed the frontiers of something that could have been his cocoon and his prison. The same stream flows through a system of communicating vessels: his hypertrophic ego, a reality experienced, dreamed of or imagined (sometimes to the point of obsession, of a myth, or of magic), a form parodying itself. This stream is called Gombrowicz. It is powerful enough to sweep away the reader, while criticism fails to imprison it in its habitual channels.

Gombrowicz's repeated but somewhat obscure variations on the themes of formlessness, immaturity, and inferiority are so many crumbs thrown to the critics. It is obvious that any conceptual criticism of his writing will miss its essence. His work was elaborated in a profound contempt for ideas, a disdain of systems and a derision of intellectual constructions. If the themes, the obsessions and the superstitious belief in 'signs' which it contains are revealed by the writer, they inevitably lead back to the man, to Gombrowicz, the civilized 'Barbarian', the dynamiter in a policeman's uniform. It is significant that, in an encounter with a generally accepted idea according to which form and content are one and the same thing for the artist, Gombrowicz should take pains to distinguish between them. Form, for him, is the sugar coating of the pill, the unobtrusive packing containing the explosive.

The man was as elusive as his work and what he says here of himself simply enhances the mystery of his character. Excessively sensitive and ridden by anxiety, he dissimulated his permanent dissatisfaction under an imperialistic ego which adopted every sort of form, from a determination to fascinate to outright aggression. Whatever the means he used, whether charm or aggressiveness, the aim was the same: to take possession of the Other, generally considered to be an adversary and sometimes an enemy, so as to force him to his knees, to have him at his mercy. When I told Gombrowicz that he would be in Berlin together with Michel Butor, who had also been awarded a Ford Foundation scholarship, he said: 'It won't take me three months to devour him'. And he was hardly joking.

I had a strained relationship with Gombrowicz until we finally broke with each other. He imagined that I had obtained a hold over him by publishing his books, and, even though I didn't dream of proclaiming myself to be his 'discoverer', he couldn't forgive me for appearing as such, for having given the first fillip which set him off on the road to fame. He had put himself in a position of 'inferiority' and the dependency which had developed in his imagination was unbearable for him. It was in vain that I assured him of my complete and sincere admiration for his work, that I put myself entirely at his service: I was always in his debt. It was *he* whom I should love, *he* for whom I should tilt, *he* whose name I should cry to the four corners of the earth; it was *he*, finally, for whom I should obtain the Nobel Prize! Unfortunately I was only a publisher—and not even that. I was the editor of a series and a literary critic, too humble a cog in the glory-making machine. So he accused me of obstructing his career, and when I 'discovered' another Pole, Bruno Schulz, Gombrowicz started to hate me, in spite of the fact that Schulz had been a friend of his, had died many years earlier and could hardly constitute a danger for him. In the biography which he wrote himself for the present work he put paid to me as his 'discoverer' once and for all.

I found out later that he had nothing against me personally. His grudge was against Poland where his works were banned, against France and Paris which had adopted him so late, against the whole world which had remained blind for so long to his genius. His aggressiveness concealed a perfectly justfiable claim in addition to an immense suffering, that of the man unrecognised and misunderstood.

His hypertrophic ego masked an 'inferiority' which he felt intensely towards the very greatest writers, towards Goethe or Shakespeare, his only and constant references. As an adolescent he had probably wanted to resemble them and he had experienced the distance between the desire and the accomplishment. He could not content himself with being Gombrowicz, one of the most original writers of our day.

One evening, when he saw me baulking at his efforts to fascinate (he was posing as the *bel esprit parisien*, which, coming from him, surprised me), he asked me point-blank: 'What do you think of me?' Unaccustomed though I am to doing so, I replied: 'You irritate me.' He scowled and fell silent. I realised that I had wounded him deeply. I was also unaware of the fact that half an hour earlier an attack of asthma had left the brilliant 'seducer' panting for breath at a street corner. The part he had played before me had been an act of courage, perhaps of heroism.

Today I take all the blame. I should have known that he, of all people, knew the world of human relationships where one man's attitude imposes itself on another's, where 'form' operates with brazen logic, a word or a feeling stamping the awaited reply on the Other's mind. In order to prove myself worthy of him I should have thwarted his provocation. He wanted my attitude to be lothsome so that he could loathe me.

The reader of this Testament, who has been spared any personal dealings with Gombrowicz, will see better than I exactly what he was: an exceptional individual, a character quite out of the common, whose work, exemplary in so many ways, will continue to be profoundly *perturbing*.

A KIND OF TESTAMENT

BIOGRAPHY OF
WITOLD GOMBROWICZ

Dictated by Witold Gombrowicz shortly before his death

1904 — 4 August. Born on his father's estate at Maloszyce, 200 kilometres south of Warsaw. His father, Jan-Onufry, was a land-owner and chairman of an industrial association. His mother, Antonina Kotkowska, was the daughter of Ignacy Kotkowski, a land-owner. He was brought up in the Catholic faith.

1906 — His parents left Maloszyce for Bodzechow, the estate of his grandfather Kotkowski. They later returned to Maloszyce.

1910 — He started studying with private tutors. French governesses taught him French. He travelled to Germany and Austria every year with his mother.

1914 — During the war Maloszyce was periodically on the German-Russian front. He saw some of the fighting, troops were stationed in his parents' house: the war made a deep impression on him.

1915 — He settled with his family in Warsaw at 3 Sluzewska Street.

He continued to study privately with two other pupils, his cousin Kotkowski and Casimir Balinski, under the surveillance of a governess. They were known as 'the trio'.

1916 — When he was fourteen he went to the Catholic lycée, St. Stanislas Kostka, which was frequented by the aristocracy.

1920 — He wrote his first work: the history of his family, based on family archives. It was never published, but was typed out.

1922 — He took his school-leaving certificate at St. Stanislas Kostka, getting uneven marks: 0 in Latin, Algebra, and Trigonometry, and full marks in Polish and French.

1923 — He read law at the University of Warsaw, but took no real interest in his studies. 'I didn't go to the lectures. My valet, who was more distinguished than I, went instead.' After some minor lung infections he had to spend several months at Zakopane, in the Tatra Mountains, or on his brother Janusz's stae, Potoczek. There, in the solitude of the forests, he started his first novel, which he destroyed immediately. It was the story of an accountant.

1926 — He stayed in Zakopane where he wrote his first real novel. He said later that it was his most original work. He then tried to write a bad novel, by using its defects rather than its qualities (melancholy, nostalgia, timidity, indolence). On the advice of his friend, Madame Szuch, he destroyed the book.

He started flirting with his cousins and his sister's girl friends who irritated him because of their excessive Catholicism. His family hoped that he would get engaged to a young Catholic countess, a friend of his sister's, two years his senior, and organized a discreet luncheon in a restaurant so that he could propose to her. But he failed to do so.

The first time he fell in love was with a girl who lived near his brother George's estate at Wsola. He used to meet her at night, risking his life by crossing a rickety little bridge and walking five miles. His affection for her lasted a few years.

He took his law degree at the University of Warsaw and then went to the Institut des Hautes Etudes Internationales in Paris. Here he stayed a year, in Rue Belloy, between Rue Kléber and Place des Etats-Unis.

He neglected his studies, his father stopped his allowance, and he started to lead a disorderly life, keeping bad company.

1927 — He left for the Pyrenees, in the south of France, after spending a year in Paris. He lived at Vemey, Boulou, Port-Vendres. He made friends with a group of people involved in the white slave trade and was almost sent to prison, but was saved by Father Barcelo, who was to become a friend of his.

He returned to Warsaw after spending six months in the Pyrenees.

1928 — In order to continue receiving an allowance from his father he strated training to become a lawyer, in the Warsaw Courts. He attended trials as a clerk and wrote reports of the proceedings. 'I couldn't tell the magistrates from the murderers, and I shook the murderers by the hand.'

He started writing short stories:

1. *Krajkowski's Dancer*

2. *The Memoirs of Stefan Czarniecki*

3. *Premeditated Murder*

4. *Virginity*

1929-1932 — He wrote other stories:

1. *The Feast at Countess Fritter's*

2. *Adventures*

3. *The Kitchen Stairs*

4. *Events on H.M.S. Banbury* (written in court)

He played tennis constantly.

1930 — He began to frequent the literary cafés.

1933 — His stories were published under the title *Memoirs of a Time of Immaturity*. This ill-chosen title gave rise to considerable confusion between him and his critics. He had a few admirers, but most serious critics thought that the book proved his immaturity.

1934 — He ended his law studies, though he had not paid much attention to them for some years. He set up his literary table at the Café Ziemianska. He started to write his play *Princess Ivona* and two short stories, *Philifor* and *Philmor*, which later became part of *Ferdydurke*.

1935 — His father died of a heart attack.

He moved to 35 Chocimska Street where he took a couple of rooms opposite the flat where his mother lived with his sister.

He inherited half the estate of Maloszyce and had a share in the rent of a block of flats belonging to his family.

Princess Ivona (Ivona, Princess of Burgundia) was published in the review *Skamander*. The critics took no notice of it and it was not performed in any theatre.

1935 — He started *Ferdydurke*, and was to spend a few hours a day on it for two years. He wrote reviews for several Warsaw papers, above all for *Kurier Poranny*, but in a rather conventional manner, without expressing his own ideas.

1936 — He continued to write *Ferdydurke*.

He went on a few journeys.

Had minor affairs with the cook and the maidservants, and a flirtation with a young and beautiful poetess.

1937 — *Ferdydurke* was published in October by Roj of Warsaw who insisted on his paying half the production costs. Violent reactions, both favourable and unfavourable. Under the pseudonym Nienaski he wrote a detective story. *The Enchanted*, in serial form for the evening paper *Express Wieczorny*.

1938 — Trip to Italy.

Long stay in the Tatra Mountains, where he rested.

1939 — He was invited by a Polish shipping company to sail on the maiden voyage of the *Chobry*, which left for Buenos Aires on 1 August. During his stay in the Argentine, war broke out. Cut off as he was from Poland, his stay in the Argentine was to last until May 1963—for twenty-four years.

1940 — He stayed in small hotels in Buenos Aires, living on his wits and borrowing money.

He wrote under a pseudonym for several papers and reviews in Buenos Aires.

1941 — He decided to settle in Buenos Aires. He learned Spanish. He had hardly anything to do with the Polish émigrés and his friends were mainly young Argentinians. Homosexual experiences with lower class boys he picked up in Buenos Aires.

He continued to write for newspapers under a pseudonym. He played chess at the Café Rex. Gradually a little group of friends formed around him.

He led a Bohemian life and wrote nothing serious. Women who believed in his work gave him some money.

He was increasingly fascinated by South America. He had a brief affair with a poet's daughter.

1944 — He started to write his play *The Marriage* in the mountains of Cordoba. At the same time he wrote a short story: *The Banquets*

1947 — *The Marriage* was published in Spanish, in Buenos Aires, by Eam. The translation and publication were financed by a rich friend of his, Cecilia Debenedetti.

He started his novel *Trans-Atlantyk*. At the same time he wrote another story, *The Rat*.

His life in the Argentine became increasingly precarious. Unwilling to return to Poland on account of the communist regime, he started to work as a secretary in the Polish Bank.

1948 — All he did at the bank was to write *Trans-Atlantyk*.

He finally broke with the Argentinian literary milieu, which he had never frequented very much and had approached largely for economic reasons. His provocative and frivolous attitude had never facilitated his relationship with the intellectuals in the capital.

1950 — He established contact with the Polish émigré review in Paris, *Kultura*, which published excerpts from his novel *Trans-Atlantyk*. These provoked the most hostile reactions.

1952 — *Trans-Atlantyk* and *The Marriage* were published in a single volume by the Polish Literary Institute (*Kultura*) in Paris. *Trans-Atlantyk* had a preface by the Polish writer Joseph Wittlin, whose authority provided him with some degree of protection.

1953 — He started to publish his diary in the review *Kultura*.

He was to continue publishing his diary, excerpt by excerpt in Polish in *Kultura* [until his death, Ed.].

1955 — He left the Polish Bank where he had worked for seven years. A bold decision, for his books earned him nothing. He managed to live thanks to a small scholarship from Free Europe and a few lectures.

He could devote himself to writing his novel *Pornografia*, and started on a musical comedy, *Operetta*.

1957 — A thaw in Poland. The liberalization of the régime. All his works were published in Poland except for his diary. His play, *Princess Ivona*, was performed in Krakow. The repercussions were enormous, and the entire edition was sold out in a few weeks.

At the same time, in Paris, François Bondy wrote an enthusiastic article on *Ferdydurke* in the review *Preuves*. Consequently Maurice Nadeau suggested including *Ferdydurke* in his series *Les Lettres Nouvelles*, published by Julliard (who had previously turned down the book, as had several other large Parisian publishers). The author paid for the translation. He received 200 dollars in advance. The first volume of his diary appeared in Polish, published by the Polish Literary Institute (*Kultura*) in Paris.

1958 — Though the success of *Ferdydurke* in Paris was confined to a certain élite, publishers began to take an interest in him, not only in France, but in the rest of Europe.

He started to be translated into all languages, with the exception of those behind the Iron Curtain, and, after 1958, he was again banned in Poland because of the change in attitude of the regime.

His health deteriorated. His first attacks of asthma.

He continued to live outside the Argentinian literary milieus, where rumours of his success in Europe were greeted somewhat sceptically.

Journey to northern Argentine and Uruguay. Stay at Tandil in the Argentine. Spent two months at Santiago del Estero during the winter.

1959 — His mother died in Poland.

1960 — The first edition of *Pornografia* was published in Polish by the Polish Literary Institute (*Kultura*) in Paris.

1961 — In February his sister died of asthma in Poland.

April. For the first time he won a literary prize, the *Kultura* Prize in Paris, worth 200 dollars.

He started his novel *Cosmos*.

Journey to Uruguay.

1962 — June. *Pornografia* appeared in French, published by Julliard in *Les Lettres Nouvelles*.

October. First edition of the diary (second volume, 1957-1961) in Polish, published by the Polish Literary Institute (*Kultura*) in Paris.

1963 — Invited to spend a year in Berlin by the Ford Foundation. On 8 April, on board the *Federico*, he left the Argentine for Europe after twenty-three and a half years.

April-May. Spent a month in Paris. 15 May. Left for Berlin.

1964 — January. The European premiere of *The Marriage* at the Théâtre Récamier in Paris, directed by the Argentinian, Jorge Lavelli.

April. Illness. Spent two months in hospital in Berlin. His asthma became worse.

From May to the end of August he spent four months in Paris and at Royaumont, where he met a young Canadian student, Marie-Rita Labrosse.

September. He left for the South of France with Marie-Rita Labrosse. He spent three weeks at La Messuguière, near Grasse. He arrived in Vence on 25 September and moved into 36, Place du Grand-Jardin [where he was to stay until 1 April 1969, shortly before his death].

December. Finished his novel *Cosmos*.

1965 — June. Spent a month in Italy, staying with his friends Maria and Bohdan Paczowski in Chiavari.

September. *Cosmos* was published in Polish by the Polish Literary Institute (*Kultura*) in Paris.

October. Premiere of *Princess Ivona* in Paris, at the Théátre de France. Directed by Jorge Lavelli.

Wrote the second version of *Operetta*.

December. Huge success of *Princess Ivona* in Stockholm, directed by Alf Sjöberg.

1966 — April. *Cosmos* published by Julliard in *Les Lettres Nouvelles* in Paris.

2 September. Finished *Operetta*,

6 November. The third volume of the diary and *Operetta* published in Polish by the Polish Literary Institute (*Kultura*) in Paris.

December. Successful production of *The Marriage* in Stockholm, directed by Alf Sjöberg.

1967 — January. His brother Janusz died in Poland.

May. International Publishers' Prize for *Cosmos*.

1968 — January. Success of *The Marriage* at the Schiller Theater in Berlin, directed by Ernst Schröder.

Entretiens de Dominique de Roux avec Witold Gombrovicz published by Pierre Belfond in Paris.

French edition of *Journal Paris-Berlin* published by Christian Bourgois in Paris.

18 November. Heart attack. Infarction of the myocardium.

28 December. Married his companion Marie-Rita Labrosse.

1969 — Recovered from his heart attack.

1 April. Moved to the Résidence Val-Clair in Vence.

[24 July. Died in Venice at midnight from a heart attack during his sleep. Ed.]

1

MY BACKGROUND

Should I talk about my life in connection with my work? I know neither my life nor my work. I trail the past behind me like the misty tail of a comet, so, as far as my work is concerned, there is not much I can say.

Darkness and magic.

You see, I have to apologize in advance. In these somewhat hasty communications I shall be unable to avoid some rather powerful words—like magic. Or darkness. I once read the memoirs of a mountaineer. He described climbing a very high and difficult mountain. Well, this description was completely distorted by the fact that the author, feeling obliged to sacrifice himself to the modesty of a sportsman, wrote: 'My left foot slipped and for ten seconds I was suspended over the chasm, until my right foot encountered a spur of rock.' Professional modesty prevented him from conveying the immensity of the chasm, the immensity of his efforts and of his fear.

In order to reassure you I shall add that in my life and work, drama and anti-drama intermingle until they are indistinguishable, just as big words are counterblanced by little ones.

Let me start with my family. It is by no means unimportant. I come from a noble family which, for some four hundred years, owned estates in Lithuania, not far from Wilno and Kovno. On account of the property it possessed, the offices it held, and the marriages it contracted, my family was slightly above the average run of Polish nobility, though it never formed part of the Aristocracy. Although I was not a count, a certain number of my aunts were countesses, but even these countesses were not of the first water—they were just so so.

In 1863 the Czar of Russia confiscated the property of my grandfather, Onufry Gombrowicz, falsely accused of having participated in the Polish uprising. With what remained of his money my grandfather purchased a small estate two hundred kilometres south of Warsaw. His son, my father, Jan, married the well-endowed daughter of Ignacy Kotkowski, the owner of the Bodzechow estate, and bought Maloszyce, where I was born.

My father was not only a landowner, he was also an industrialist. He started off at Bodzechow as manager of a paper mill which belonged to my grandfather Kotkowski, and was then given other jobs in the management of some larger factories.

So, in that Proustian epoch at the beginning of the century, we were a displaced family whose social status was far from clear, living between Lithuania and the former Congress Kingdom of Poland, between land and industry, between what is known as 'good society' and another, more middle-class society. These were the first 'betweens', which subsequently multiplied until they almost constituted my country of residence, my true home.

My father? Handsome, tall, distinguished, very proper, punctual, methodical, not very broad-minded or artistic, a practising Catholic, but no bigot. My mother, on the other hand, was extremely vivacious, sensitive, imaginative, lazy, indolent, nervous, almost too nervous, riddled with complexes, phobias, illusions. (The Kotkowski family had numerous mental diseases. When I stayed with my grandmother in the country I was almost frightened out of my wits: the large, low house was divided into two parts, one inhabited by my grandmother, the other by her son, my mother's brother, an incurable lunatic who paced the empty rooms at night, trying to overcome his terror by strange monologues which gradually turned into curious chants and ended in inhuman screams. That lasted all night. The atmosphere was pervaded by insanity.)

I am an artist because of my mother. I inherited my father's lucidity, his level-headedness, and his sense of discipline. But my mother also had an extremely irritating characteristic—yes, she was one of those people who are incapable of seeing themselves as they are. Worse still—she firmly believed herself to be the very opposite of what she was—and that had something provocative about it.

By nature she was, as I said, lazy and bereft of any practical sense. However, in those Proustian days, there was a quantity of servants; the French governess looked after the children and my mother simply gave orders to the cook, the maid, or the gardener. But that didn't stop her saying that she had 'the whole household on her hands', that work was 'ennobling', that 'the garden at Maloszyce is all my own work', and 'fortunately, *I* have a practical mind'.

'In my spare moments I like to read Spencer and Fichte', she would say in all sincerity, although the works of these philosophers occupied the lower shelves of the library, their uncut pages gleaming.

You see, *by nature she was*	*but she imagined herself to be*
impulsive, naïve	rational, lucid
capricious	disciplined
cultured in a very worldly way	intellectual
anarchistic	organized
nervous	courageous
greedy	frugal
comfort-loving	ascetic, even heroic

She had nothing but admiration for everything she was not. She was fascinated by eminent doctors, professors, great thinkers, and by serious people in general. Her ideal was the mother with intangible (Catholic) principles who concentrated on her duties and sacrificed herself for her family. She identified herself with what she admired with a truly remarkable naïvety.

It was she who pushed me into pure nonsensicality, into the absurd, which was later to become one of the most important elements of my art.

We, the boys (there were three of us, my two brothers and I, the favourite), rapidly discovered the best way to torment and tease her. We simply had to say, systematically, the opposite of whatever she might say. My brother Jerzy and I soon became masters at it. My mother only needed to say 'the sun is shining' for us to reply in amazement, 'What? Go on with you! It's raining.'

'You've got a mania for saying silly things!' she would answer indignantly, but Jerzy would continue in a conciliatory manner: 'Let's say that it isn't raining, but that it might rain!' And I added, after a moment's thought: 'Let's say that it isn't raining, but that if it started to rain it would be raining'.

This sport, which consisted in dragging our mother into absurd discussions, was one of my first introductions to the world of art (and dialectics). Since she was passionately attached to 'religion' and the 'family, that nucleus of society', she severely condemned divorce, which unfortunately abounded in our world. So, of course, Jerzy shouted: 'Another divorce in the family', as he took off his coat in the hall. She didn't answer, because she smelt a rat. From the other room I shouted back: 'What's that? Another divorce in the family? That's not possible!' 'Oh yes, it is. I've just seen Aunt Rosa who told me, under oath of secrecy, that the Henryks were going to get a divorce. She's fallen in love with her hairdresser'. 'How shocking!' I said, and, finally, my mother rose to her feet, trembling: 'If Henryk's wife is so cynical, we're not going to invite her here any more!' 'But why not?' we replied. 'Aunt Ela has been divorced three times and plays bridge with her three husbands. Apparently they make a perfect team. One can't deny that divorce has its brighter sides. She says that it's procured twice as many parents for her children. . . . '

Arguments about divorce continued year in year out, they never ceased, they thrived on their own grotesqueness. How divinely absurd! It was at such a school that I learned to support nonsense heroically, to insist solemnly on stupidity, to celebrate cretinism piously. . . . Ah, Form! The divine idiocies of my writing, which never cease to amaze me, this capacity to combine stupidity with the most rigorous logic, all originated in these discussions.

She never even suspected what a remarkable teacher she was! Nothing was healthier, more educational, more character- and intelligence-forming than her terrifying defects. For me she was a school of values. Exasperated to the point of madness by her self-deception, I heightened my sense of quality of value, which is at the basis of every work of art. Art is the choice of the best, the rejection of whatever is less good. It is founded on the most rigorous hierarchy of values, on a continual process of valorization. I then began to understand about the critical spirit, objective judgement, distance, the refusal to yield to facile and comfortable illusions. It was without a drop of pity, without love, full of a glacial irony, how I played with my mother for several years.

She was devoted to me.

It was from her that I inherited my cult of reality. I consider myself a dedicated realist. One of the main objects of my writing is to cut a path through Unreality to Reality. I believe that she was the first chimera with which I got to grips.

There is no doubt that my mother was, as the Marxists say, conditioned by her social environment. And nothing is more surprising than the fact that, through her deception, I should have discovered, somewhat precociously, the most shameful aspect of my family: our life was easy! The servants! The servants! They knew what life was about. They were the ones who really worked, while we simply ate the roasted geese. We were the consumers. The refined delicacies of 'good society', epicureanism, the love of comfort, sybaritism, idleness, all these things struck me when I was only ten.

Here's a scene which often comes back to me: a farmhand in a pea-jacket, his head bare under the rain, talking to my brother Janusz, wearing a coat and sheltered under an umbrella. The hardness of the farm-hand's eyes, his cheeks, his mouth, in the pouring rain . . . Beauty. . . .

But perhaps, had it not been for my 'guard', I would never, in later life, have plunged into degradation. This guard was composed of boys of my age, the sons of the farmhands, a sort of regiment which I commanded. But they rode better, they climbed trees better, they jumped and ran better than I did. I was the worst, but I was their leader. I had a recurring dream during this period: Maloszyce,—they, the 'guard', lay on the lawn in front of the house waiting for me, and I wandered through the entire building, I went up to the windows, peeped out at them, hid behind the curtains, went from room to room, to other windows, watched them, but could never go out and join them!

It was during the First World War. I think the front lines must have run past our house about four times, back and forth, back and forth, the booming of the canon in the distance, then coming nearer and nearer, buildings on fire, armies fleeing, armies advancing, bombardments, corpses near the pond, and Russian, Austrian, German detachments stationed in our house. We boys used to pick up the bullets, the bayonets, the belts, the cartridge clips. The fumes of brutality were pervasive, exciting, although the world of the masters to which I belonged saved me from direct contact with the war.

Yes, I hated the drawing-room. I secretly adored the pantry, the kitchen, the stables, the stable lads, the farm girls—what a Marxist I was then!—and my sexual instincts, which were aroused early, were nourished by war, violence, soldiers' songs and sweat. It bound me to those soiled and laborious bodies. Degradation became my ideal for ever. If I worshipped anybody, it was the slave. But I didn't realize that by worshipping the slave I became an aristocrat. . . .

As you see, if I take a bird's eye view of my youth I can distinguish, by and large, certain initiations, and even define a certain ground on which my life was to be enacted. The cult of the absurd, the relationship between reality and unreality, superiority and inferiority, master and slave, already obsessed me. And there was another thing: even then I led a double life. Within me I felt something obscure which nothing could bring to the light of day. Besides, I was quite incapable of loving. Love was refused me, once and for all, from the start, but was that because I couldn't give it a form, an expression of its own, or because I didn't have it in me? I don't know. Was it lacking or did I strangle it? Or maybe my mother strangled it. Or else. . . . One never remembers the past clearly, dispassionately. The present is always too aggressive, even when life is waning, and the more this present life is moulded, polished, defined, the further it plunges into the troubled waters of the past in order to fish out what alone can be of use to it in the present and can improve its present form. Maybe I don't remember the past very well, and simply devour it in order to feed what I am today.

2

MY FIRST WORKS

My first works to have given me any satisfaction were the short stories *Krajkowski's Dancer*, *The Memoirs of Stefan Czarniecki*, *Virginity*, and *Premeditated Murder*. I wrote them when I was twenty-four or twenty-five and they have been assembled in the complete collection of my short stories, *Bakakai*.

I had tried to write since the age of sixteen. My early works were extraordinarily uneven. They were naïve and awkward at a time when I was neither that naïve nor that awkward myself. My pen betrayed me, and I suffered because of it. I was on the verge of despair and, when I was about twenty, I decided to write a deliberately 'bad' novel, to be inspired by all that was bad, shameful, inadmissible in me. That might well have been my most courageous—and my most important—work. . . . But I gave a typed copy of it to a lady whom I trusted and who believed in me. She read it, returned it to me without a word, and refused to see me any more. In a panic I threw the manuscript into the fire: nothing remains of it.

A few years elapsed and I wrote *Krajkowski's Dancer*. It seemed good to me. I realized that it was literature, and after that I started writing seriously.

I sometimes wonder why I chose one particular style of writing rather than another. I adopted a fantastic, eccentric and bizarre tone from the very start—why? Why did my style immediately break with normal reality, why did it border on mania, folly, absurdity—even if this absurdity did not lack a certain solemn logic? Well, I had been trained to do this, as I said, by my conversations with my mother. But that isn't a good enough reason and there is no doubt that this aristocratic form, infatuated by its own splendour, ran parallel to my own private, shameful miseries. Painful and agonizing. . . . To use the words of one of my protagonists. 'Day by day my position on the European continent became increasingly precarious and equivocal.'

But to return to my youth. . . . I always found myself 'between' things. I never fitted into anything.

I was sent to school in Warsaw, a Catholic school full of young princes and counts. My brothers and I were overcome by snobbery—it was almost inevitable in our little world—and yet, strangely enough, we were not sufficiently stupid to be unaware of the absurdity and vanity of it. But for us it became a mania—or rather a game—and this ridiculous mythology caught us in its grip. It would no longer release us! Odd! Odd! Because we weren't snobs, and now, when I look at our life closely, I see that none of us made any effort in that direction. Janusz liked to live on his own in the country. Jerzy played bridge with anybody, and I was far too lazy and negligent to enter those distinguished drawing-rooms. Odd! Because we were snobs in spite of it all, although we were not really snobs. Ah! Form!

I grew older. In three different respects, which had nothing in common with each other.

To start with, I was a boy of 'good family', polite, fairly healthy, neither ugly nor handsome, passable, flirting with his cousins, neither a good nor a bad pupil, rather a mother's darling, delicate, anxious, and at the same time bantering, chattering, often unbearable at school, bullied by his older school mates, sociable, frivolous, bold or shy according to the occasion.

Secondly I was an atheist and an intellectual, already flirting with art. The separation from God—a moment of intense importance, when the mind opens itself to the totality of the universe—took place without my noticing it, I don't know how it happened. Quite simply, towards my fourteenth or fifteenth year, I stopped worrying about God. But I don't think he worried me much earlier, either. As far as the intellect was concerned, I was still in the first form (aged fifteen) when I started glancing at the *Critique of Pure Reason*. I have kept the notes which I made at the time on synthetic *a priori* judgements, on Spencer, Kant, Schopenhauer, Nietzsche, Shakespeare, Goethe, Montaigne, Pascal, Rabelais. . . .

I was looking for a style, a style that displayed thought and a basic sensibility, a style which reflected independence, liberty, sincerity, and, perhaps, mastery and control. I devoured these writers' styles, their way of expressing themselves, their tone, their deportment, voraciously. But I was awkward . . . I had a certain rustic clumsiness . . . I was handicapped by the naïvety of the landed gentry and by Slavic effusiveness. I felt silly.

Thirdly, I was abnormal, twisted, degenerate, abominable, and solitary. I slunk along, hugging the walls. Where could I find this secret blemish, which separated me from the human herd? In physical illness? But, except for some minor lung infections, quite common among boys of my age (which caused me to go to the mountains for a month or two), I was in reasonably good health. . . . So what could be the cause of this inner disorder, which turned a reasonably happy boy like me into a bizarre monster, lured by deformity, by all existing aberrations? I was—and I realized this without the slightest astonishment, without so much as a hint of protest—an abnormal being who could never admit to anybody what he really was, condemned to hide forever, to conspire. Erotic impulses dragged me downwards, towards the gutter, towards secret and solitary affairs in distant suburbs of Warsaw with girls of the worst kind. No, they were not whores. In these clumsy little affairs I looked for health, for something very elementary, something low and therefore very authentic.

But what could I do when even that changed into something grotesque the minute it touched my poisoned hands? I returned from those wild expeditions to my respectable existence as mother's darling, to the innocence of a little boy of 'good family'. How could both these aspects coexist in me? Some of my friends and I had founded a touring club, and we organized perfectly decent and proper excursions into the country. How could I devote myself to these two forms of excursion? How were these things reconciled within me? The answer is that they were not. Neither of these two realities was more real than the other. I was fully immersed in both of them and I was in neither one nor the other. I was 'between'. And I was an actor.

Life continued slowly, discontinuously, moodily, far from politics and ideologies. I was alone, I lived in private. Secretly. Out on a limb.

Hidden.

When, in 1920 (I was sixteen) the Bolsheviks broke through and arrived at the gates of Warsaw, I was appointed to some auxiliary service in the army. Far from being in any way fired by this experience, I felt glacially objective . . . and this pushed me to still further extremes. . . .

I left school. I got my diploma (only just, though, I only scraped from one class to another, but I did pass). What was I to do? I decided to study law at the University of Warsaw. Not that law interested me, but so that I could go on extracting money from my father. I completed my law studies in Warsaw—without too much difficulty—and again: what was I to do? I put myself down for the Institut des Hautes Etudes Internationales in Paris. That period in Paris, then on the French beaches, in the eastern Pyrenees, is a black hole. I can hardly remember a thing and, when I look back at it, it is as though I were looking into a well . . . I can't make out a thing, not a thing—I recall certain scenes, images, flashes, but it is as though I wasn't there, as though I was lost. This inner disorder which I had felt for so long may well have reached its highest pitch. How can I define my state of mind? I don't think it was so much that I felt abnormal as that I *knew* myself to be abnormal, and this knowledge persisted despite all the signs of my healthy normality: a young man, apparently perfectly average (except for a few inoffensive eccentricities) and yet under no illusion about being a black sheep, outside the fold, on a road that led nowhere—a young man who knew himself to be open to all possibilities, even the most grotesque, like those plasticine figurines which can be modelled indefinitely and turned into the most hideous monsters. I knew: alone, out on a limb, like this or like something else, dissolute and uncontrolled. That was the source of my relationship with all that is repugnant, disgusting, and horrible—for, though it disgusted me, yet I felt drawn to it, not to say attached to it. But this sensation plunged me into still greater disgust until I felt as uneasy as if I had received a piece of bread from someone else's hand. So I oscillated between disgust and an inner attachment to all that was disgusting. Had I not been naturally cowardly ('prudent', said my friends, ironically), had I not been frightened of the police, I might even have committed some very serious crimes . . . but I was afraid. Am I not exaggerating? There must have been something in this French period of my life, something corrupt. It is not natural that it should all be so veiled for me. Of course, I may well have been slightly insane in that period (I inherited certain propensities from my mother).

In these circumstances, whatever French culture might have to offer me ran off my back like water. In that long night, however, there remains one dazzling moment: my discovery of the south. I remember it well. I was in the Pyrenees, somewhere near the sea, playing billiards with some young workmen who suggested we should go to the beach. They gave me a bicycle and we started racing down a road which led to the sea. What with the speed, the oranges, the wine, the light, the glare, everything became as hard as a diamond . . . the south was revealed to my northern spirit. When we arrived I was so intoxicated that I was unable to stop my bicycle, and raced around the square in circles.

But I already had the south in my blood, and I greeted it with joy, with relief, with hope, not like something precious in itself but like a new principle which brings with it a new possibility. Is that why I subsequently decided to spend my life in the Argentine? Was the Argentine already contained in it? I become a little mystical when I gaze at my past. . . .

My 'prudence' did not prevent me from falling into bad company, from seeing people who had indulged in shady little deals, connected with smuggling from Africa to France, and though my conscience was quite clean, one morning I had to clear out. My friends were having difficulties with the police. I returned to Poland. What was I to do? I had no idea. I wanted to be a writer. But not that much.

In order to continue living at my father's expense (I was incapable of earning my own living) I began working as a law clerk. As such I had to attend the sessions and draw up reports. Not much to do, one session a week. That was when I wrote the stories I mentioned earlier, and added four more to them: *The Feast at Countess Fritter's*, *Adventure*, *The Kitchen Stairs*, and *Events on H.M.S. Banbury*. Except for *The Kitchen Stairs* I submitted them (with shame) to a publisher.

These stories appeared in 1933 in a volume entitled *Memoirs of a Time of Immaturity*. This was my first book—a little work aspiring to brilliance, a glinting trifle of fantasy, invention, humour, irony. Today, when I re-read these stories from the distant past, I say to myself, well, they *are* full of astonishing contrasts, unexpected visions, humour, and games!

Fair enough. But let's admit that these pages contain a certain element that is morbid, revolting, repugnant.

By all means. Let's also admit that these revolting elements lose their repugnance when they turn into elements of Form.

They serve Form, their role is functional, they follow a superior aim: artistic creation.

So 1 agree. That slimy pulp of Formlessness in me spilled onto the book—but not to spread like a stinking puddle, no, not at all! In order, rather, to shine with all the colours of the rainbow, to gleam with humour, to ennoble with poetry, and to attain to divine innocence in absurdity. If you ask me how I regard these stories today I would say that they serve as an acquittal, perhaps even as an absolution.

At the beginning of my literary career, Form appeared as an absolving, almost divine force. In other words I could carry in myself all the abominations of the world but, if I knew how to play with them, I was their lord and master.

In real life I was anxious, uncertain, indolent, a prey to anarchy, lost. On paper I wanted to be brilliant, funny, triumphant . . . but above all pure. Purified.

And yet you will say that there is something which is not authentic in this book. Its dirtiness is not really dirty, its innocence not really innocent. It escapes reality. This is quite true. I could go further than parody. The parody of reality and art. Ever since my childhood, the falsity of my easy, bourgeois life had been a nightmare for me. This feeling of unreality never left me. Always 'between' and never 'in',

I was like a shade, a chimera. And I would not be lying if I said that it was reality for which I searched in the simplicity and the brute health of the lowest social classes, during those expeditions into the slums of Warsaw. But I also looked for that reality inside myself, in those vague internal areas, deserted, peripheral, inhuman, where anomalies flourish together with Formlessness, Disease, Abjection. For one can find reality in all that is most ordinary, most primitive, and most healthy, as well as in what is most twisted and demented. Man's reality is the reality both of health and of disease.

Yet these investigations did not go so far as to make me touch the depths of things. So I wasn't entitled to write a 'real' book. I was capable of no more than parody. Here style was the parody of style. Art mimicked and mocked art. The logic of nonsense was a parody of sense and of logic. And my so-called success was a parody of success.

It proved most fruitful that, instead of starting with a work which strove to be sincere, serious, and authentic, I yielded to such fun and games.

If these stories had been serious, sincere, and authentic, I would have been lying simply because I was incapable of sincerity and lying is unhealthy for an artist.

Besides, parody allowed me to liberate Form, to tear it from weightiness and launch it into pure space, where it became light, bold, and revealing. I must add that at this time I knew nothing about Joyce or Kafka. I hardly knew a thing about surrealism and I only had a very vague idea about Freud. If I managed to catch something of all that, it was only because it was in the air, in conversations, even in jokes. The formal apparatus which I had put into motion was mainly of my own invention. And this apparatus unexpectedly led me into regions where I would never have ventured if I had not got so drunk on the absurd, on games, mystification, and parody. Look at stories like *H.M.S. Banbury* or *Adventures* or any other, and you will find situations, intuitions, visions which are in no way inferior to those I achieved subsequently. It must be admitted that, within certain limitations, this first book often reached the same level as my most successful works.

I later wrote *Philifor* and *Philimor*, *The Rat* and *The Banquet*, which were technically more accomplished but which did not differ essentially from the preceding stories. *Philifor* was the triumph of the Function over the Idea: it was based on Symmetry. *The Rat* was extraordinarily introverted, and *The Banquet*, progressing from pianissimo to fortissimo, reached real heights of power.

What did I get out of my first book? Hardly anything— and at the same time a great deal—for the whole thing was a game.

Memoirs of a Time of Immaturity was an ill-chosen title. I had thought it would help the sales, but it also concealed the naïveté of the landed gentleman. Just when I was panic-stricken, I wanted people to know that I had written the book like that, because one has to start somehow, that it was only a sample, a prelude to something better. (I was very ashamed of writing at the time. I hid my papers when anyone entered my room, I wrote in secret, and, even today, I am as much embarrassed by the cheek of young writers who claim proudly: 'I am a poet', as by the vainglorious parade of such established figures as Cocteau and Aragon.)

Memoirs of a Time of Immaturity appeared in 1933 and, when I went out into the street that day, I knew that something decisive had happened to me.

I had shown a typed copy of the stories to my friends, Tadeusz Breza, Adas Mauersberger, and his sister, Toni Sobanski. They had received them very well, so I had people who believed in me from the start—and others joined them. But these were only private opinions. The reviews in the papers began to accumulate: 'This young writer has not yet learnt how to express himself.' 'Gombrowicz was right to emphasize his immaturity in the title.' 'The author lapses into a pretentious hermeticism.' 'Let us hope that one day Mr. Gombrowicz will grow more serious.'

It was as though they had danced on my face! I beat a retreat, dazed and frightened. Darkness. . . . For the first time I felt for myself the effects of literary criticism which is, and will remain, for the most part, nothing but a donkey braying through the loudspeaker of the press.

Suddenly the worst intellectual-artistic mob of Warsaw-cultivated old gossips, 'connoisseurs', casuists, and 'guardians of values' paid a penny a line sprayed me with hasty, superficial, condescending, and rather stupid verdicts.

I was an object, so there was nothing I could do.

Not all the reviews were so bad. But I had enough to feel that my most precious qualities had been treated lightly. So what could the encouragement of certain enthusiasts do for me? The papers denounced my immaturity. 'Witold has been flayed', said my family, aggrieved.

3

IVONA

However that may be, *Memoirs of a Time of Immaturity* opened the doors to artistic society. It procured me a certain prestige in *avant-garde* circles. I started frequenting the literary cafes of Warsaw, but I was never in the best company. The group of poets known as 'Skamander' and their weekly review *Wiadomosci Literackie* were the vanguard of the younger generation. It was in their wake that one gleaned honours and obtained publicity. I never joined the table of the Skamanderites—maybe because of my boorish shyness, maybe because I didn't want to appear as a novice, or maybe because I wanted to be master of my own house. In short I treated myself to my own table, an unusual table where candidates and babes sucking the nipples of art took their place, provincials, dishevelled thinkers, starving young poets, ragged dreamers, the whole level raised by a few true talents . . . and I held forth before this circle with an unruly obstinacy, with an admirable and steely constancy. Evening after evening, night after night, I said and repeated the silliest things. But at the same time they were not really silly because somewhere, in some way, they were my truths.

Keep up my style, that was my supreme principle. Of course, I never gave the impression of taking myself too seriously and I even went out of my way not to give the impression of being serious. Bewitched as I was by Form, I was prepared to become its buffoon forever.

In this period I met the brilliant Bruno Schulz (who is all too little known in the West) together with Adolf Rudnicki. Most of my intellectual friends were Jews and it was they who constituted the majority of my audience. I was sometimes even called the king of the Jews. I owe a great deal to them.

But . . . what could I do? I still didn't feel strong enough to submit to my fate. In order to gain time I wrote a play, and this is how *Ivona, Princess of Burgundia*, came into existence.

Ivona was to surprise me. When it was published, in 1935 if I remember rightly, in the Skamander review, it attracted no attention and the pre-war Polish theatre took no interest in it. (I then adopted the fad of despising famous actresses and, in order to humiliate them, I introduced myself whenever I came across one of them. One day, at a party, after I had introduced myself to her for the fifth time, an actress seized a glass of water and hurled it in my face, saying: 'Now you'll remember me!' Not the best way of entering theatrical circles, perhaps. . . .)

In short, *Ivona* passed unnoticed in pre-war Poland and, when the war broke out and I found myself in the Argentine, I almost forgot about it too. Its success in Paris, Stockholm and elsewhere almost twenty years later, fell on me like ripe fruit from a tree. It came as an unexpected aid in the hard battle waged by my novels.

The tragicomic history of *Ivona* can be summed up in a

few words. Prince Philip, the heir to the throne, meets this charmless and unattractive girl as he goes for a walk. Ivona is awkward, apathetic, anaemic, shy, nervous, and boring. From the start the prince cannot stand her, she irritates him too much; but at the same time he cannot bear to see himself obliged to hate the wretched Ivona. He suddenly rebels against those laws of nature which order young men only to love seductive girls. 'I won't stand for it, I'll love her!' He defies the laws of nature and gets engaged to Ivona.

Introduced to the court as the prince's fiancée, Ivona becomes a decomposing agent. The mute, frightened presence of her innumerable deficiencies reveals to each courtier his own blemishes, his own vices, his own dirtiness. . . . In a short time the court turns into an incubator of monsters. And each monster, including the fiancé, longs to murder the unbearable Ivona. Finally, the court mobilizes its pomp, its superiority, and its splendour, and with full grandeur, kills her.

That's the story of *Ivona*. Is it so hard to understand? I'm ready to admit that I am unlucky and that, therefore, all that is clearest and most simple in my works is received in the most complicated and aberrant manner. Even today I occasionally come across reviews of *Ivona* which treat the play as a political satire against the present Polish regime—*Ivona* is identified with Poland or liberty—or as a satire against monarchy. Well! Be that as it may. Other things need to be emphasized: to start with *Ivona* is more a product of biology than of sociology; and then, she originated in that region within me where I was assailed by the limitless anarchy of form, of human form, of its dissoluteness and licentiousness. So it was always within me . . . and I was within it. . . .

4

FERDYDURKE

Ivona was not what I needed, you know. It was only a game, a way of winning time. Time passed. I was in my thirties. And day by day, my position on the European continent became increasingly precarious and equivocal. What could I do? How could I link my writing with the reality of my existence?

This is the same question that I ask myself today, now that I am in my decline . . . *eternal retour!* Anyhow, let's take a closer look at a work which was born out of this question thirty years ago: the novel, or rather, the pamphlet entitled *Ferdydurke*.

The defence of my personality. I knew what I had to write. I had to defend myself, to impose myself, to fight for myself! This new work had to serve me personally. And this was to be the guarantee of its being rooted in reality. Because, I thought, reality, this general, objective reality, is not reality at all. True reality is the one which is peculiar to *you*.

I cannot write 'Tomato soup is good.' How misleading! But I am entitled to say 'I like tomato soup.' That's how we must talk! That's style.

My work must become myself.

Immaturity. It always moves me when I discover the presence of a certain tenacious logic in the chaos of my existence.

You know this already: I was composed of at least three beings—one was a country gentleman, naive, boorish, a mother's darling. At the last moment this panic-stricken country gentleman, myself, gave my book the clumsy title *Memoirs of a Time of Immaturity*. Consequently the critics exclaimed joyfully: 'Look at him! He isn't mature!'

So, when I tackled *Ferdydurke*, I picked up this accusation of immaturity. Immaturity—what a compromising, disagreeable word!—became my war cry.

Had it not been for the title of my first book I might never have become the poet of immaturity, or the poet of Form . . . at least in its connection with immaturity.

Chance? Not really. This title was not chosen by chance. It was not by chance that my awkward, compromising self seized that glittering little volume and made my mark on it. This is how my little book was *enriched* . . . by that part of my 'self' which had to remain secret.

Ferdydurke *does not want to defend me*. Yes, I shall defend myself. I shall mock the mockers! Immature? Me? It is your stupidity which brands me as immature! So, all of a sudden, along came teacher Pimko. He called on me, chatted about this and that and then suddenly made me take an exam! He took me for a schoolboy! He gave me a bad mark! And finally, having given me, a thirty-year-old, a childish little slap on the behind, he led me triumphantly off to school!

I can well remember that, when I started *Ferdydurke*, I wanted to write no more than a biting satire which would put me in a superior position over my enemies.

But my words were soon whirled away in a violent dance, they took the bit between their teeth and galloped towards a grotesque lunacy with such speed that I had to rewrite the first part of the book in order to give it the same grotesque intensity. I felt that *Ferdydurke* was escaping me, that it didn't want to serve me. It started living a life of its own, governing itself according to laws of its own, and, instead of aiming at my enemies, it was dragging me off somewhere else.

You know, it is not without pleasure that I can tell my majestic colleagues who write for humanity, and in the name of humanity, that I have never written a single word other than for a selfish purpose; but, each time, the work betrayed me and escaped from me.

This is what happened to *Ferdydurke*.

But what *did* happen?

Let us try to reply as simply as possible. Why did a work born out of such personal injuries drag me into so universal an adventure as the drama of human Form, as the ferocious battle between man and his own Form (that is to say his battle against his way of being, feeling, thinking, talking, acting, against his culture, his ideas, and his ideologies, his convictions, his creeds . . . against everything by which he appears to the outer world)?

Ferdydurke was supposed to defend my personality. But which one of my multiple personalities?

I repeat: 'Day by day my position on the European continent

became increasingly precarious and equivocal'.

Well! We already know that I was an agglomeration of different worlds, neither one thing nor the other. Indefinite. If I were followed step by step and spied on, my every contact with people could easily show just how much of a chameleon I was. According to the place, the people, the circumstances, I was good, stupid, primitive, refined, taciturn, talkative, self-effacing, arrogant, superficial, or profound. I was agile, heavy, important, unimportant, bashful, shameless, bold or shy, cynical or idealistic. What was I not? I was everything.

What a lack of maturity! Maybe I should give a few examples of the gaffes I committed in those days.

Here is one of them: a few months after my stories had been published I collected the most flattering reviews in order to distribute them among my friends and acquaintances. They were entitled 'Reviews of *Memoirs of a Time of Immaturity* up to . . . (here I put the date).' Isn't that 'up to . . . ' touching?

How could a man who was almost thirty, who had just written a provocative *avant-garde* book which was by no means childish, behave so childishly? It was with similar ineptitude that I became the victim of those low-brow critics against whom I had to fight for my own maturity.

My father died. When thanking someone for his condolences, I made an ink stain on my letter. I posted the letter with the stain . . . as if to say that at such a tragic moment stains are unimportant.

I still blush when I think of it. I limit myself to such trifles intentionally. But how great is their power if I can still blush at them thirty years later!

How could such a man hope to be satirical, critical, superior, sure of himself? And how could he hope to conquer his enemies?

Better still. Had I been followed step by step into the corners of suburban lanes, the surprise would have been even greater . . . caused blushes. By the time I was thirty I had not had one single normal love affair. For reasons unknown to me I did not want love. I loathed it. My eroticism was tragic, physical. I was always searching blindly for something precious which I knew could only be found on the lowest levels of life. The erotic impulse inevitably dragged me down. In my most elevated enterprises, I never rose above a little love affair of a light, amusing, friendly nature—while at my lowest . . . That's enough. Let us leave the splendours of that misery. So, if had I been caught in certain situations someone quite unexpected would have been discovered, someone gifted with an astonishing facility maybe, but with other eyes and other hands, a criminal, perhaps, or someone frivolous or disarming . . . *Sapenti sat.*

I could add a hundred more, two hundred more shades to my personality . . . each one independent of the others, following a path of its own.

Of what literary expression would I be capable? How could I fend for myself in these conditions?

A Frenchman or an Englishman never experiences such lack of harmony—at least not to this extent. Whatever a Frenchman or an Englishman might feel individually, even if he is profoundly torn within himself, he will always seek refuge in a certain national, English or French, form, which has been elaborated over the centuries.

I was Polish.

The passages in my diary where I mention 'Polishness' have only been read very superficially by western readers. I was almost told: 'You'd better cut all that. What has that got to do with us?' It is high time that the heirs of superior cultures stopped turning up their noses. Instead of 'Poland' put the Argentine, Canada, Romania, and so on, and you'll see that my allusions (and my sufferings) can be applied to most of the globe. They concern all secondary European cultures. Look at them still closer: you'll see that they constitute a poison which may affect *you* too.

I was Polish. I happened to be in Poland. What is Poland?

It is a country between the East and the West, where Europe starts to draw to an end, a border country where the East and the West soften into each other. A country of weakened forms . . . None of the great movements of European culture has ever really penetrated Poland, not the Renaissance, not the wars of religion, not the French Revolution, not the Industrial Revolution. Of all these phenomena Poland has felt no more than a muted echo. And the contemporary Russian revolution hasn't really been experienced there either, its prefabricated results have simply been (forcibly) imposed. Catholicism? The country is admittedly in the orbit of the Vatican, but Polish Catholicism is passive, it is limited to a rigorous observance of the catechism; it has never collaborated creatively with the Church.

So those plains, open to every wind, had long been the scene of a great compromise between Form and its Degradation. Everything was effaced, disintegrated. . . . Poland, deprived of those great cities (and their bourgeoisie) where life can be concentrated and complicated, where it can arise and flourish, had a rural, peasant culture, yes, a culture represented by squires and priests. The nobleman sitting in his farmstead made the peasant do the work, and the village priest was the oracle. This feeling of formlessness tortured the Poles, but at the same time it gave them a strange sense of liberty. It was one of the basic causes of their admiration for their 'Polishness'.

Please understand the additional difficulty of my position, compared with that of other western writers. Had I been bom in France or England I would have known how to behave better!

And how, in my fight for my identity, could I lean on my national cultural tradition?

Of course there was a Polish form—a fairly obvious one, Sarmatian style! But it was not very substantial; it already contained a destructive fragility. Where was the original Polish thought, Polish philosophy, Polish intellectual and spiritual participation in European creativity? For a hundred and fifty years literature had been stifled by the trauma of our loss of independence—it was reduced to the dimensions of our local misfortune. Mickiewicz[*] was the greatest figure in Polish literature. How could I base myself on Mickiewicz, a magnificent poet, but whose views and ideas were those of a pious child lost in an ingenuous mysticism? Could I fend

---

[*] Adam Bernard Mickiewicz (1798-1855), Polish playwright, poet, and novelist. In 1822, he published a book of verse, *Ballady i romanse,* which has been described as heralding the Polish romantic movement. He also wrote the poetic drama *Dziady* in 1827; two poetic novels, *Grazyna* (1927) and *Konrad Wallenrod* (1828); and his masterpiece *Pan Tadeusz* (1834).

for myself by leaning on him? We only have to compare Mickiewicz with Goethe to realize how absurd such a plan was.

Most Polish writers of my generation could choose between two alternatives. They could limit themselves to Polish ground, but were thereby condemned to play a secondary role; or they could aspire to a European role, but in this case they were still condemned to a secondary role, because they were merely second-hand Europeans, they could only try to equal Europe and to repeat Europe.

But why not try to join the major currents of the period, you might ask me. They, too, are homelands, in a certain sense. If not Catholicism, then Communism or Fascism.

Catholicism, me, an unbeliever?

Communism or Fascism, me, an unbeliever?

No, I had no vocation to become a monk who believes, who is afraid of not believing, who does not admit any doubts and who goads himself on in his faith. Theories? Ideas? I always knew that they were sieves through which life runs. And the role of the 'committed', progressive intellectual teaching humanity which path to take seemed to me both too pretentious and too frivolous. I want to tell you about my life as simply as possible, so here I shall give the least complicated of my arguments: where, I asked, is the certificate that entitles me to guide humanity? And what if I am a fool who simply botches everything and makes other people's positive work more arduous? Is history not full of high-minded individuals whose indomitable high-mindedness has caused countless squabbles and has led to interminable brawls? So—mind your own business and don't go sticking your nose into other people's. You see, for me, the postulate which consisted of speaking only in my own personal name was not simply the elementary prerequisite of a good style: it also proved my moral sense, my sense of responsibility (and, as usual, this has been wrongly interpreted: my moral scruples have been attributed to my aridity, to my selfishness and my arrogance).

Besides . . . How could I, a Pole, believe in theories? That would be grotesque. Against the Polish sky, against the sky of a paling, waning Europe, one can see why so much paper coming from the West falls to the ground, into the mud, onto the sand, so that little boys grazing their cows can make the usual use of it. But these theories, which drift across the sky, become ridiculous, blind, ignoble, bloody, vain. Gentle ideas are pregnant with mountains of corpses. What can one do? Everyone sees the world from where he stands. It is not for nothing that I come from the plains which separate Europe from the rest of the world.

Communism, Fascism, the Church, any particular faith? No.

All on my own, without any support, racked by doubts, I didn't know what to do. What could I do? I was only sure of one thing: it was solely by cutting it that I could escape from this Gordian knot. This idea of total intransigence, which had occurred to me, had existed somewhere inside me ever since my childhood. It was even connected with a certain optimism, at least as far as literature is concerned. Because I—and I was sure of that, immature though I was—had a right to speak. I had a right to express myself, like everything that exists, like everything that is. You see, I had what everyone has: I knew what one might call the language of fact.

What could I do? To start with, I told myself, I must acknowledge this state of affairs. I must acknowledge reality and bring it to light.

If, as a man, as a Pole, and an artist, I was doomed to imperfection, there was no point in my grinning and bearing it, in my pretending, to myself and to everybody else, that everything was getting better and better. To break, once and for all, with mystification, was a matter of honesty, dignity, lucidity, and vitality.

Let us start with Poland. I had to break with Poland and turn against it. Like France for the French, Poland for the Poles is a treasure wothy of the greatest sacrifice. Well, it was absolutely necessary to state that Poland, that intermediary creature between the East and West, was doomed, by its geographical position and by its historical development, to imperfection, to a minor role, and that Poland must be passed over because it could not guarantee any fully authentic value for the Poles. It is not right that a Pole should sacrifice all his individual development, all his humanity, to Poland. The Pole, formed by Poland, by the Polish environment and tradition, is necessarily a less sophsticated man than the westerner. One can understand how a Frenchman might dedicate himself to adoring France, an Englishman to adoring England. These countries have provided their natives with precious advantages. But to be a man is more significant than to be a Frenchman, and Europe is more significant than England and France. So, for men situated in minor, weaker countries, like Poland, the Argentine, Norway, or

Holland, and bound to them sentimentally, subjugated by them, formed by them, it was really a matter of life and death to break away, to keep one's distance. . . .

No, even 'constructive' criticism of one's country's faults—undertaken in a patriotic spirit, in order to improve it—was no longer sufficient. Such criticism was itself conditioned by the country. To break away! To keep one's distance! The writer, the artist, or anyone who attaches importance to his spiritual development, must feel no more than a resident in Poland or the Argentine, and it is his duty to regard Poland or the Argentine as an obstacle, almost as an enemy. That is the only way to feel *really* free. And only those people for whom their country is an obstacle rather than an advantage will have a chance of becoming truly free spiritually, and, in the case of Europe, truly European.

So, these were my views then, but I elaborated on them as time went by.

Well, I wanted to be like those young men one sees in the stations of small provincial towns, their packs in their hands. They are just about to leave, and when they see the train which is to take them away, they murmur: 'Yes, I must leave my birthplace. It's too small for me. Farewell! I may return, but not before the wide world has given birth to me again.' 'After that I shall no longer be Polish! I shall be all on my own.'

'On your own? But loneliness will deliver you up to your own misery!'

'Give me a knife, then! I must perform a still more radical operation! I must amputate myself from myself!'

I suppose that Nietzsche might have formulated my dilemma in these terms. I proceeded to amputate. The following thought was the scalpel: accept, understand that you are not yourself, that no one is ever himself with anyone, in any situation, that to be a man is to be artificial.

Is that simple enough? Yes, there was only one difficulty. It was not sufficient to accept it and to understand it, I had to experience it.

History came to my assistance. In the pre-war days something odd was happening to people. I saw with amazement how, with the war, Europe, particularly central and eastern Europe, entered a demoniacal period of formal mobilization. The Nazis and the Communists fashioned menacing, fanatical masks for themselves; the fabrication of faiths, enthusiasms, and ideals resembled the fabrication of canons and bombs. Blind obedience and blind faith had become essential, and not only in the barracks. People were artificially putting themselves into artificial states, and everything—even, and above all, reality—had to be sacrificed in order to obtain strength. What was all that? Glaring idiocies, cynicial falsifications, the most obvious distortions of reality, a nightmarish atmosphere. . . . Monstrous horror. . . .

These pre-war years were possibly more damaging than the war itself. Suffocating under this pressure I leapt as energetically as I could towards a new understanding of man—this was the only hope. Where was I? I was in the darkest of nights, together with the whole of humanity. The old God was dying. The laws, the principles, the customs which had constituted the patrimony of humanity were suspended in space, despoiled of their authority. Man, bereft of God, liberated and solitary, began to forge himself through other men. . . . It was Form and nothing else which was at the basis of these convulsions. Modern man was characterized by a new attitude towards Form. How much more easily he created himself, created as he was by it!

I imagined the men of the future forming each other deliberately: a shy man will find people who make him bold; by skilfully manoeuvring others and himself, a roué will obtain a good dose of asceticism.

I added my private experience to this general view of humanity and I derived a measure of tranquility from it. I was not the only chameleon. Everybody was a chameleon. It was the new human condition, and one would have to face up to it.

I became 'the poet of form'.

I amputated myself from myself.

I discovered man's reality in this unreality to which he is condemned.

And *Ferdydurke*, instead of serving me, became a fantastic poem describing, as Schulz said, the tortures of man on a Procrustean bed, the bed of Form.

I may be oversimplifying, if only by presenting this mental process as something decreed in advance, previous to the composition of *Ferdydurke*.

To tell the truth, the artist doesn't think, if by 'thinking' we mean the elaboration of a chain of concepts. In him thought is born from contact with the matter which it forms, like something auxiliary, like the demands of matter itself, like the requirement of a form in the process of being born. Truth is less important to the artist than that his work should succeed, that it should come to life. My 'thoughts' were formed together with my work, they gnawed their way perversely and tenaciously into a world which gradually revealed itself.

It is partly because of this that the artist's 'thought', however lame it might sometimes appear if compared with the thinker's thought, is often taken seriously. His thought is not a dry and abstract deduction, it is born from the desire to make something live, to create something living . . . and real . . . so it is deeply rooted in life.

I shall quote a few excerpts from a chapter of *Ferdydurke*[*] which act as a sort of commentary to the novel:

> Let the cry be backwards! I foresee that the general retreat will soon be sounded. The son of man will realize that he is not expressing himself in harmony with his true nature, but in an artificial manner painfully inflicted on him from outside, either by other men or by circumstances. He will then begin to fear this Form that is his own, and to be ashamed of it as he was previously proud of it and sought stability in it. We shall soon begin to be afraid of ourselves and our personalities, because we shall discover that they do not completely belong to us. And instead of bellowing and shouting: I believe this, I feel that, I am this, I stand for that, we shall say more humbly: In me there is a belief, a feeling, a thought, I am the vehicle for such-and-such an action, production, or whatever it may be . . . The poet will repudiate his song, the commander will tremble at his own orders, the priest will fear his altar, mothers will no longer be satisfied

---

[*] Translated by Eric Mosbacher.

with teaching their children principles, but will also teach them how to evade them, to prevent them from being stifled by them.

And:

Great discoveries will have to be made, great blows will have to be struck with our poor bare hands against the tough armour-plate of Form. Unparalleled cunning, great honesty of thought, and intelligence sharpened to a degree, will be required to enable man to escape from his stiff exterior . . .

And:

Try to set yourself against Form, try to shake free of it.

Ferydurke appeared at the end of 1937. My relations with people changed. I undoubtedly felt much better. In a certain sense this book established me.

I felt better, but never had I felt so ill. Sad, depressed, exhausted, I spent a few months in the Tatra Mountains, and then left for Rome. Giving birth to a book is never agreeable, but this birth was the most agonizing experience I have ever known. Besides, I was periodically obsessed by the most banal fears, for *Ferdydurke* was quite a provocation (something I forgot when I was actually writing it) and the nationalist press attacked me brutally, accusing me of having a corrupting influence. This meant that I might well have been beaten up by Fascist gangs. I had already suffered considerably at school for, despite my cowardice, I was forever provoking people.

Seriously. There were the painful and difficult moments when I heard people ask me, 'Well then?' and I heard myself reply, 'Nothing, nothing.' These moments have always obsessed me when one of my books was about to appear— but never so much as then. Nevertheless, during my stay in Rome, where I didn't meet one single Italian writer, where I hardly had anything to do with anybody, where I simply roamed through the streets without so much as glancing into the churches or the museums, something characteristic happened to me which proved that *Ferdydurke* had not been written in vain. This is more or less what occurred.

Before St. Peter's I met one of those painters who go to Rome in order to study, a Pole from Lithuania. The painter asked me: 'Have you visited the basilica yet?' I replied: 'No, all churches are the same inside.'

'You think so?'

He was ironical. I knew why. For a painter or a writer from the countries of degraded Form, from the frontier zones of Europe, the journey to Paris, Rome, or London adopted the proportions of an important problem. How was he to behave? How should he adapt himself? Calm respect and discretion? Cold politeness? Admiration? Humility? The shameless irony of the demi-barbarian? Familiarity? Cynicism? Premeditated simplicity? All those tactics only have one fault: they betray a violent inferiority complex. And unfortunately this inferiority complex is incurable simply because it is not a complex, but reality . . . the reality, I should add, of the poor relations.

Somebody ingenuous might say that it was enough to forget oneself and yield to the contemplation of works of art. Hollow dreams! One cannot forget oneself.

I knew how to interpret his ironical 'You think so?' That meant: 'Ah! So you've chosen nonchalance and contempt.'

I replied that that was what I thought and besides, I couldn't be bothered to take my hat off before going into a church.

'Well then, go in with your hat on.'

To this I answered: 'That's not a bad idea. I'll go in with my hat on.'

The rest of the conversation is unimportant. What mattered very much was that, as I said all this, I did not feel in any way idiotic! This phrase, which he no doubt regarded as a piece of buffoonery, a pose, a means of 'saving one's face' at all costs, sounded perfectly natural to me, it sounded sincere and self-assured . . . and, as I said that, I felt European. I felt as much at ease as anyone who had ever walked past that venerable basilica. I felt at home. Why? Thanks to *Ferdydurke*, I had a part to play in Europe. What part? Well, it was up to me to tell that church, those madonnas, that Roman forum, those frescoes and libraries: 'You are man's equipment and nothing else'. After *Ferdydurke*, you see, I really had the right to go into a church with my hat on, and it wouldn't be a mere prank, but a conscious act, having nothing in common with Communism or Nazism, or any Dadaism or Surrealism. I was entitled to do it. And, after that, throughout my life, during twenty-three years of the Argentinian pampas or anywhere else, I never lost the certainty that I was European, more European, perhaps, than the Europeans of Rome or Paris. I was virtually sure that the revision of European Form could only be undertaken from an extra-European position, from where it is slacker and less perfect. The profound conviction that the imperfect is superior to the perfect (because it is more constructive) was one of the basic intuitions in *Ferdydurke*.

What liberty, then! And how satisfying to talk on equal terms to the madonnas, to approach the masterpieces disrespectfully, to have the whole of Rome at my feet, like something too narrow in its majesty! And all the various tendencies of my soul, starting with my attraction towards degradation, my 'squire-like' distrust of art, and my secret relationship with Formlessness, contributed to this heretical aggression. Later, when *Ferdydurke* was translated into other languages, I realized to what an extent its disrespect could irritate certain cultivated Germans or Frenchmen or all other representatives of western maturity. Some exclaimed: 'How idiotic!' and threw the book into the wastepaper basket. The book can be quite indigestible for those who attribute a certain importance to their person, their convictions and their beliefs, for a 'dedicated' painter, scientist, or ideologist. The western readers of *Ferdydurke* are divided as follows: frivolous individuals who amuse themselves without worrying about anything else; serious readers; serious and offended readers.

I returned from Rome to Warsaw via Venice and Vienna. If this were a novel and not an account of my life I would describe my return as follows: I travelled triumphantly, in order to tell the Poles, 'Hear ye! Hear ye! I proclaim victory! I have conquered Rome and Europe! And each of you will do the same if, after reading *Ferdydurke*, you will abandon your Polishness!'

But bang! In Vienna my train ran into crowds of people, torch-lit demonstrations . . . Hitler had arrived! The Anschluss! In Warsaw, the excitement, the crowds, the feverish state of alarm. . . . And now Poland had once again to lock itself in, like a fortress, to believe in itself, to love itself! And from every country there came the panic-stricken fury of threatened peoples. Mobilization!

What became of my Roman holiday, my triumph, before this new and monstrous tension? Was I not ultimately in contradiction with my time?

In all events I understood one thing: *Ferdydurke* was doomed to failure and myself with it.

It was only ten years later, after the universal catastrophe, that *Ferdydurke* and I began to give further signs of life on the ruins and the ashes of Form.

Bruno's lecture. I may have spoken too much about the East and the West, Poland and Europe. But this is because I am writing for western readers. And, by the same token, the western reader will no doubt be particularly struck by my 'inferiority complex' with regard to the West. But no! Don't simplify the task, gentlemen! I repeat: I am not talking about complexes but about something far more serious—about real inferiority and real superiority.

It is time for me to say that the release which *Ferdydurke* became for me was not limited to these matters. Other matters were contained in it, seethed in it—more arduous, more confidential matters.

At about the time when I was on the point of entering St. Peter's with my hat on, my eminent friend Bruno Schulz (all too little known in the West) arrived in Warsaw from western Galicia to give a lecture on *Ferdydurke* at the Society of Men of Letters. This lecture aroused a chorus of protests from the protectors of 'mature Polish literature', which proved, at least, that my pamphlet was capable of provoking a tempest in a teacup. In his lecture Bruno presented one of the deepest analyses of *Ferdydurke* that has ever been made—I must emphasize this, because it all happened in the old days, before the flood.

Amongst other things Bruno spoke of 'the zone of subculture' revealed by my novel, of its 'apparatus of secondary forms'.

This means that in *Ferdydurke* a shameful inner world is revealed which can only be confessed to and formulated with the greatest difficulty. Yet this world is not the Freudian world of instinct and the subconscious. It is the result of the following process: in our relations with other people we want to be cultivated, superior, mature, so we use the language of maturity and we talk about, for instance, Beauty, Goodness, Truth. . . . But, within our own confidential, intimate reality, we feel nothing but inadequacy, immaturity; and then our private ideals collapse, and we create a private mythology for ourselves, which is also basically a culture, but a shabby, inferior culture, degraded to the level of our own inadequacy. This world, said Bruno, is composed of the remains of the official banquet: it is as though we were simultaneously at table and under the table.

Take the ideal of feminine beauty in *Ferdydurke*. My Venus is a modem schoolgirl who fascinates you with her calves, while another god of this sub-mythology is the lowly farm-hand with whom Mientus wants to fra . . . ternize (not simply fraternize, but fra . . . ternize, become a brother, which is far worse). *Ferdydurke* is full of these *immature* ideals, of these inferior myths, of these second-class beauties, of these shoddy charms and dubious graces. . . .

Schulz emphasized that this world is not born so much out of the liberation of instinct as out of the degradation of Form. On the outside we want to be as cultured as possible . . . but, because of this very fact, within ourselves, we are below the level of our own culture . . . and we drag it downwards, down to our real level. . . .

> There is no titivating or decadent enough an ideology, no paltry or tedious enough a form for it not to have its value and find its buyer. Here all the structures of mythology appear in their most lurid light—the dissimulated tyranny of syntactical forms, the violence and banditry of ready-made phraseologies, the power of symmetry and analogy.

And he continued:

> Gombrowicz did not follow the smooth path of intellectual speculation but the path of pathology, of his own pathology.

This was true.

We later had a discussion during which he reproached me bitterly for not being up to what I wrote. Seated on my chair, I murmured something innocently, but, in my heart of hearts, I knew he was right. I wasn't up to it. I, the specialist of inferiority, was inferior to my novel—I, the private individual, the landed gent Gombrowicz. Why couldn't I celebrate victory? My accursed pathology. Yet I had ripped it out of myself, it was in the book, it was simply the subject matter of *Ferdydurke* and no longer myself. So pride yourself, author! You have disinterred your deepest shames, you have cast them from you. And now, transformed into a 'zone of sub-culture', your dustbin has become your claim to fame. So pride yourself, inventor of the zone of sub-culture!

Ugh!

I was seated on a chair. A fly. You know, there is a great injustice in artistic creation. You write in the terror of seeing yourself dishonoured by failure, and you are right, because the failure of a work is a great personal disgrace. But, if the work is more or less successful, you won't reap any personal profit from it, or even, I dare say, any personal satisfaction. A successful work lives a life of its own, it exists somewhere, on the side, and there's not much it can do for the life of its author.

A fly. Exactly the same thing was happening to *Ferdydurke* and myself as happened, in its pages, to my protagonists. The work, transformed into culture, hovered in the sky, while I remained below. Maybe I preferred it like that, maybe that suited me better, maybe I felt better in my farmyard. A fly. And then what? And perhaps (as I have already noted in my diary), perhaps my immaturity, my youth were more precious to me.

5

FORM

My view of Form has often been interpreted somewhat narrowly by my readers and critics. It is generally reduced to the idea that men shape each other. This is a little too simple. Of course, I haven't organized things into a system. I'm not a scientist. All I can do is to refer to some of the situations in my books.

To start with let us say that the deformation produced between men is not the only deformation, if only because man, in his deepest essence, possesses something which I would call 'the Formal Imperative'. Something which is, it seems to me, indispensable to any organic creation. For instance, take our innate need to complete incomplete Form: every Form that has been started requires a complement. When I say A, something compels me to say B, and so on. This need to develop, to complete, because of a certain logic inherent in Form, plays an important part in my work. In *Cosmos*, the story is made up of certain Forms which start off as embryos, insinuate themselves into the book, and gradually become increasingly distinct . . . like the idea of hanging. My hero is on their trail. He thirsts for them, lusts after them, he thinks that something is going to emerge, that the puzzle is going to be . . . solved . . . he's afraid of this, but he wants it . . . and each time Form relapses into chaos.

The same Formal Imperative recurs in the story of the two professors in *Ferdydurke*. It is the imperative of symmetry and analogy. The professor of higher synthesis finds his pendant in the professor of higher analysis, one acts synthetically, the other analytically. The demon of symmetry, present throughout the story, reaches his apogee during the duel scene. When the analyst moves away from the axis of symmetry by pulling the little finger of Professor Philifor's bride, the synthesist has to move away in his turn by pulling the little finger of his opponent's mistress.

One critic rightly defined this story as the triumph of the 'function' over the 'idea'. In the end both the ideas of 'higher synthesis' and 'higher analysis' become mere pretexts for the pure pleasure of action. As, I assume, does Fascism or Communism.

Yet this imperative of Form often leads to far more complex and perverse situations in my work. In *Cosmos*, my hero notices a whole string of anomalies, minimal and imprecise. Each of them, taken on its own, has hardly any significance. But, when they are strung together, they give the impression of meaning something . . . a sparrow hung on a wire, a piece of wood hung on a thread, arrows on the ceiling pointing in a certain direction, a shaft . . . which might also be pointing somewhere. . . .

And all this, supported by my hero's further adventures, by his fatal love for Lena, begins to appear like an ever more insistent hanging . . . whose hanging? Lena's? At one point my hero, overcome with impatience, anxious to end the charade, adds a hanging of his own to the chain: he hangs the cat he has just strangled on a hook. It is a treacherous and perverse act, because it overflows from the inner world to the outer world: it is as though he was besieging himself. But it springs from a profound spiritual necessity.

I was only conscious of what I was writing up to a point. My works seem to form in me just as reality forms in them. Other elements collaborate in me too, and I am not always aware of them. Where, for example, did I get that 'physical distance' from in the second part of *Cosmos*? Or the 'echo'? Why did I make my characters leave for the mountain? And the finger stuck in the mouth . . . first of the corpse, then of the priest?

The obvious nature of these scenes may have irritated some readers. From an artistic point of view the obvious is desirable. The process of man's creation of Form will be all the more distinct, the more it compels him to perform terrible, savage, eccentric acts. In order to become entirely tangible he must cross the border of normality.

Why does the hero of *Cosmos* stick his finger into the hanged man's mouth? To establish—he is well aware of it—a link between 'hanging' and 'the mouth'. Until then it had all been situated on two different levels. The association which tormented him to the point of madness between Lena's mouth and Katasia's horrible mouth could not be connected with this idea of 'hanging' which obsessed him at the same time. From then on, thanks to this act, he connects them in himself. Why? To be able to hang Lena? All that has matured in him for a long time. Obviously a whole mass of poisonous impulses can be concealed in such an act. The finger in the mouth can have a sexual significance, and so on. There are various possible interpretations. What matters to me is that there are acts which we perform not for external motives, but because we feel the necessity of connecting them with certain associations, with a certain organization of reality. These are the acts we perform on ourselves.

You know, in *Cosmos* I tried to isolate the deep current of Form so that it should appear as such, like a black river following its own course, opaque and troubled, concealing ever new and unfathomable potentialities. In my mind it was originally a very dramatic work, and I should think that this is how it will appear in the future…that is, when our direct perception of Form as a creative force will have asserted itself. We will then understand how terrible its dynamism is.

Ha! The adventures of Form are numberless. In a comic chapter of *Ferdydurke* entitled 'Introduction to Philimor Honeycombed with Childishness' I mentioned cases like 'psychological dislocation' and 'sub-human greenness'.

It would be interesting for someone to take the trouble to classify all my adventures with Form. He may find rules of which I am unaware. I let my imagination carry me away and classifications do not amuse me.

But it is very difficult to isolate the significance of particular cases: they only appear in a certain context, against a background of their own. Is putting one's finger into a corpse's mouth as 'illicit' a procedure as the hanging of the cat which preceded it? No—because it is no longer the same man who stands before the corpse. He is already 'on the other side', on the side of creation aware of itself. With the cat it was only a matter of an obscure and clumsy trial. But by now he knows what he needs. He has become bolder. He wants to be capable of hanging Lena.

The analyses which certain critics have made of my work according to the rules of structuralism have never fully convinced me. Some time ago I read a very serious analysis of *Pornografia* accompanied by a diagram. The author claimed that the main character of the book was Skuziak, the country boy whom Frederick kills at the last moment, almost gratuitously, without a concrete motive. He said that that was my most successful device, that I surpassed romantic form and that I gave the novel a new dimension. He said that I had introduced the act of writing the novel into the novel I was writing.

Yet I must admit that the forms of the novel do not interest me particularly. It seems to me typical of over-refined cultures, like Parisian culture, to tend to reduce the gigantic problem of Form to the elaboration of ever new models of the *nouveau roman*, to literature, and, worse still, to literature about literature. I know that it's their way of searching for a writer's reality, but I don't think it gets us very far. Here's another antinomy: he alone will know what Form is who never moves a step away from the full intensity of the whirlwind of life.

As far as I'm concerned, Frederick kills Skuziak for the very same reason that we put a piece of beef into our broth; to make it taste better. He wants to make it tastier, he requires the savour of a murdered boy. He acts like a theatrical producer. Besides, that was the part he was playing from the start. He wants to reach different 'realities', unforeseen charms and beauties, by selecting people, by forming new combinations between the young and the old—a sort of Christopher Columbus who isn't searching for America, but for a new reality, a new poetry. This boy, Skuziak, is a marginal figure, we don't know what he's doing here. He must be connected with the situation. But how? By being killed. It's a rhyme added to the poem, but a rhyme for the sake of rhyme and for no other reason.

The author of this study rightly pointed out that, in this sense, the act is exceptional, that it breaks away from the normal course of the novel. But if you think that I was racking my brains about the structure of the novel as I wrote the book, you're mistaken! What a boring idea! This perspicacious analyst would have done better to emphasize my delight and my confusion before the cruel charm of young blood. We must understand all the real tensions that exist between youth and ourselves. To transpose poetry into diagrams is a thankless task. If I did that I'd be ashamed of myself.

But let us return to the distinction I mentioned earlier. I emphasized that apart from the deformations which people impose on each other there is a deformation which takes place all on its own and which is the result of that Formal Imperative which rules us. So far we have talked about isolated man. I shall now talk about man among men. But I do not want to say too much about this subject. I would rather it emerged gradually, in the course of this book.

Briefly: the man who imposes his form is active. He is the subject of form, it is he who creates it. But when his Form, in contact with the form of others, undergoes a deformation, he is, to a certain extent, created by others—he becomes an object. And that is by no means a superficial transformation, because Form penetrates us to the marrow. We only have to change our tone of voice for certain things within ourselves to become inexpressible—we can no longer think them, or even feel them.

An infinity of variations impose themselves on the mind—all individuals are different, the combinations between them are inexhaustible. To this we must add the colossal pressure of pre-established Form elaborated by culture. Each of the three parts of *Ferdydurke* ends in an explosion brought about by the clash of irreconcilable Forms. The characters involved in these situations do not have the same denominators, they never accede to an interpretation or to a formula which enables them to grasp the situation. Hence the outburst of Discordance, Formlessness, and Dissolution.

Some people have found that the most interesting of these three explosions in *Ferdydurke* is the middle one, with the modern schoolgirl. This part of the book, they say, has something prophetic about it. They find it hard to believe that it was written thirty years ago because today, for the first time, 'modern youth' has been deified. Yet this was only the beginning. I shall make another prophecy: in the future youth will impose itself on our sensibility in a still more profound and terrible manner, we will see everything through the eyes of the young.[*]

The hero of *Ferdydurke* is violently prejudiced against the charms of the modern schoolgirl because they are the result

***

[*] These lines were written in December 1967, that is to say some months before the students' revolt in the East and the West. Editor's note.

of a shoddy, superficial, and immature mythology. His tactics are to confront the schoolgirl with something that is beyond her. The schoolgirl worshipped by the elderly Pimko? Yes. The schoolgirl in the arms of the youthful Kopeida? Yes. But the schoolgirl naked before both Pimko and Kopeida, that's stupid, awkward, it cannot be enclosed in a ready-made mold, particularly since the girl's parents arrive and cause still greater confusion! It all falls to pieces.

And earlier, in order to mar the schoolgirl, my hero had torn off a fly's wings and had put the mutilated fly, twitching with pain, into her room. According to his calculations the schoolgirl would be unable to bear the fly because the pain, the suffering, the horror of the world would find no place in her modern style, in the victorious and optimistic style of youth and modernity.

If someone told me that there was very little difference between this and a mere outrage of convention, like going to a dinner party without a tie on, I might agree, in order to avoid an argument. Only in my work this assumes a greater weight, it becomes the tool with which man is shaped. I would not be surprised if the artist of tomorrow were to expand his creative possibilities by means of methods such as these, by means of similar confrontations and deflagrations in the kingdom of Form.

Besides, the examples I have just given are only the first letters of an alphabet which knows no end. What a powerful and unfathomable dynamism! Man submitted to the inter-human is like a twig on a rough sea: he bobs up and down, plunges into the raging waters, slides gently along the surface of the luminous waves, he is engulfed by rhymes and vertiginous rhythms, and loses himself in unforeseen perspectives. Through Form, penetrated to the marrow by other men, he emerges more powerful than himself, a stranger to himself. Unsuspected paths appear and he sometimes no longer knows what is happening to him. He becomes a function of the tensions which arise, unstable situations brought about by men, among men, and which are the results of various impulses. This interhuman creation, unknown and unseizable, determines his possibilities.

There would be a great deal more to say about this.

I do not regard myself as a psychologist in the scientific sense of the term. Nothing of the sort. I observe and I describe. I suppose that in science it would be easy to find various views of man which correspond in some way to mine, but not one of them would be identical to mine. Theory is no problem for the artist. Theory only interests him in as much as he can make it run in his blood.

Critics have often seen me as a moralist. What place, you might ask, does morality hold in my world of unstable and impenetrable Forms? How can I reconcile an extreme relativism in my vision of man with a moral postulate? As far as I'm concerned, morality is indispensable in literature. Without morality, literature would not exist. In a sense, morality is the writer's sex appeal. Immorality is repulsive and art must be attractive. This might sound morally immoral—but it is just a little contrast, a little paradox, of which there are so many in art. Antinomies. . . .

But I really want to be moral!

Only, in my universe this question becomes fairly complicated. Our present moral sense is essentially individualistic. It always proceeds from the idea of the immortal soul, different in each man. So it is hardly ever in harmony with a human world, based on the creation of man by men. We see, more and more clearly, that something is wrong. Across how many different sets of morals do we have to make our way? There is one set of morals for a priest, another for a woman. One for the army, another for civilians. Blind obedience, which is the essence of the military ethic, is the negation of civic morality. At home, in our family, we would be incapable of killing a fly, but from our aeroplanes we drop napalm onto little children. Our epoch is alive with incidents in which morals experience curious misadventures. Back from the concentration camp the executioner fondles his little dog and listens to the nightingales, while his wife innocently places a shade made of human skin on the lamp. Are they really monsters? No, it is not as easy as that. Something is wrong somewhere.

Our condemnation, our moral indignation misfires. . . . It is not so simple. There is no one rule for all these realities . . . except for a rule so general that it can be applied every-where and thereby loses any consistency. We might have to acknowledge that what we call 'the moral being' or 'the soul' does not really belong to an individual but is composed of various human beings.

I don't know if we can talk of morals in this sense. I can't have an answer to everything. A writer is expected to provide a ready-made model of the world. I repeat that I wrote in my diary: The purpose of literature is not to solve problems but to set them. Let us console ourselves: to become aware of a problem is often the first step towards solving it.

I too tried to construct theories. And it worked quite well. I told myself: if Form deforms us, then the moral postulate requires us to face the consequences. To be myself, to defend myself from deformity, to keep my distance from my feelings, my most private thoughts, whenever they do not really express me. This is the first moral obligation.

It's simple, isn't it?

But here's the rub: if I am always an artefact, always defined by others and by culture as well as by my own formal necessities, where should I look for my 'self'? Who am I really and to what extent *am* I? This question, which is increasingly relevant to contemporary thought, troubled me at the time I was writing *Ferdydurke*. So it is as though the novel oscillated round an inaccessible centre, although, from the first to the last word, it endeavours to be the assertion of an identity.

I have only found one answer: I don't know who I really am, but I suffer when I am deformed. So at least I know what I am not. My 'self' is nothing but my will to be myself.

A measly palliative! Another formula!

Fortunately you know that I am not a theoretician but an artist. The artist is not rational and consequential. He lets off steam. Everything happens at once in the artist, everything collaborates, theory with practice, thought with passion, life with evaluation and the understanding of life, the desire for personal success with the requirements of the work in progress, the requirements of the work with universal truth, beauty, virtue. Nothing can hope to dominate the rest, everything is interdependent, as in every living organism.

These various ways of approaching things, the fact that the artist sits on several chairs at the same time, allow him a far greater freedom of action.

When I realized that theories led me nowhere I withdrew into practical life. Enough sophisms! One must put the morals one has at one's disposal to some use as they are, unless one can invent another set. To attack what one despises, what one detests, violence, falsity, cruelty, every crime, as it presents itself, without worrying about deep motives. I create myself through my work. To start with I shall fight, and then I shall see what I am.

There was undoubtedly a contradiction at the very root of my artistic efforts. By questioning Form, my works, themselves the products of Form, defined me more and more. But contradiction, which is the philosopher's death, is the artist's life. Let us repeat this: one can never emphasize it sufficiently: art is born out of contradiction.

And the morality of writing is ultimately summed up in one of the most elementary maxims, a maxim so elementary that it is almost embarrassing to formulate it: write in such a way that your reader will see you as an honest man. No more. Just that. But isn't that how people have written ever since the beginning of time? Literature and art rest more on their glorious tradition than on any rational, consequential ideas.

No, morality is not lacking in my work. But perhaps it is not I who am moral, perhaps it is my works. The moral aggressiveness of *Ferdydurke* almost astonished me. No, I didn't expect it from myself. The morality of my works is stronger than I am. I don't cultivate it, it governs me.

Am I a moral man? Yes . . . but . . . I am far too cowardly, too much of a physical coward. I can't say that I regard the fact of having put up with twenty years of misery and loneliness in the Argentine, in order not to betray my artistic principles or make any concessions, as moral victory. It happened of its own accord.

The moralizing tendency of post-war literature—of the Marxists, the Existentialists, the Catholics, Sartre, Camus, Mauriac, and so on—never convinced me. It was too dry, too stiff, it didn't inspire confidence. As far as Marxism is concerned I cannot see the point of that self-violation practised by men who are bourgeois by birth and education and who try to identify themselves with the proletariat by invoking a doctrine. That's all hot air!

And luxury. . . . These interminable analyses, these archi-subtle states of mind, these over-dramatic scruples, this mania for splitting hairs, all smell of luxury, and the smell of luxury is not the odour of sanctity. It is rather like the great trials that excite public opinion, 'You've condemned an innocent man!' But while a fortunate man becomes the subject of ardent discussions, investigations, expert opinions, and appeals which can drag on for years, hundreds of little crooks are dealt with in half an hour because there are ten other cases awaiting trial. It is almost impossible to separate a certain too moral morality from luxury, from refinement, from a high standard of living. This aristocratic morality, this secure morality, this morality in white gloves . . . bothers me. I would prefer it to be pedestrian, simple, unpretentiously dressed, a face in a crowd, a little lost in the wave of events, more immediate and less obtrusive.

Besides, luxury appears to be connected still more closely with morals on a practical level. What did morals get for Mauriac? Fame, the Académie Française, the Nobel Prize, a fairly large income, I should imagine. Isn't it because of his moral code that Sartre had such an influence on the younger generation? So morals can guarantee personal success. Haven't the representatives of Communist ethics, like Aragon and Neruda, secured extremely enviable positions in the immoral capitalist system—fine houses, decorations, chauffeurs, admirers, bathrooms, affection, and expensive furniture? Didn't Camus' moral anguish get him the Nobel Prize when he was barely over forty?

I don't condemn them, I understand them. I too would like to have fine houses, and valuable collections like Neruda. But there is nothing one can do about it—morality, for the artist, is a sort of sex appeal. He seduces and embellishes himself with it—himself and his work. So it would be better if art did not confront this delicate problem without the necessary discretion. An explicitly moralizing or excessively high-minded form of art irritates me. Of course, the writer must be moral, but he must also talk about something else. His morality must give birth to itself, in the margin of the work.

Perhaps my highest moral aim is to weaken all the structures of premeditated morality and other interhuman dependencies so that our immediate and most moral reflexes can say a word of their own. Moral constructors will no doubt consider me destructive, but what can I do about that?

I am generally classified as a pessimist, even a 'catastrophist'. Critics have grown accustomed to thinking that contemporary literature of a certain standard must necessarily be black. Mine is not black. On the contrary, it is more of a reaction against the sardonic-apocalyptic tone currently in fashion. I am like the baritone in the Choral Symphony: 'Friends, enough of this song. Let more joyous melodies be heard!' That doesn't mean, of course, that I sing paeans of joy! But I have had enough of these modern groans. The primary task of creative literature is to rejuvenate our problems.

Of all outdated problems, death seems to me the most hackneyed. If we change our standpoint slightly we only have to think: no, there is nothing dramatic about it, we have adapted ourselves to death since birth. And though it eats into us day by day we never actually look it in the face because, according to a well-known and perfectly correct aphorism, when it appears we are no longer there. Alienation? No, let us try to admit that this alienation is not so bad, that we have it in our fingers as pianists say—in our disciplined, technical fingers which, apart from alienation, give the workers almost as many free and marvellous holidays a year as work days. Emptiness? The absurdity of existence? Nothingness? Don't let's exaggerate! A god or ideals are not necessary to discover supreme values. We only have to go for three days without eating anything for a crumb to become our supreme goal: it is our needs that are at the basis of our values, of the sense and order of our life. Atomic bombs? Some centuries ago we died before we were thirty—plagues, poverty, witches, hell, purgatory, tortures . . . haven't your conquests gone to your head? Have you forgotten what you were yesterday?

Ow! It almost embarrasses me to express such simple thoughts, I don't feel equal to it.

I won't protest against a tragic vision of existence, I don't paint the world pink. But one can't go on repeating the same thing. I await a change of tone from the younger generation. They must stop being 'desperate' and 'in revolt'! The most tragic trait of great tragedies is that they give rise to little tragedies and, in our case, to boredom, monotony, and a somewhat shallow and unvaried imitation of profundity. 'Friends, enough of this song. Let more joyous melodies be heard.'

6

THE ARGENTINE

After *Ferdydurke* my work was interrupted. For ten years. It wasn't until 1947 that *The Marriage* appeared. These ten years consist of two years of pre-war Poland, then the war and the Argentine.

I left for the Argentine a month before the war broke out and remained there twenty-three years. It all happened by chance. Chance? One day at the Zodiac, a café in Warsaw, I met a writer of my age called Czeslaw Straszewicz. He said: 'I'm going to South America.' 'How?' 'In a month's time, the new Polish trans-Atlantic liner *Chrobry* leaves for Buenos Aires. It'll be her maiden voyage. I've been invited as a writer, to do a few columns for the papers.' 'Do you think they might invite me too?' 'You can always try. I'll suggest you. Who knows? It might work. The journey will be more fun if there are two of us.'

It worked. I sometimes read in the papers that I went to the Argentine in order to escape from the war. Not at all! I prepared for the journey quite casually and it was thanks to chance alone (chance?) that I didn't remain in Poland.

The day before I left, I was all ready, all my papers were in order, and I went to the café. 'You have got permission from the military authorities, haven't you?' someone said. 'I've got my passport. I presented all the military certificates I could, otherwise I wouldn't have got it.' 'That's not enough! You need a special permit from the military authorities. It's only a formality, but they won't let you board the ship without it.'

I looked at my watch. Twenty to seven. The army offices shut at seven. I jumped into a taxi and rushed up to the fourth floor. Too late. The doors were shut. It was three minutes past seven. I knocked all the same. The doorman appeared. 'The office is closed. Please stop that noise.'

The door closed onced more. Farewell America! I started down the stairs gloomily: suddenly, downstairs, a terrible din. It was a football team leaving for an international match in Denmark. They'd arrived late too. We knocked again. This time, the doorman let us in and, as a special favour, we were given the necessary stamps. You see, my twenty-three years in the Argentine all depended on a few minutes.

What with all this business about leaving, it was as though an enormous hand has seized me by the collar, lifted me out of Poland, and placed me in this lost land in the middle of the ocean—lost, but European . . . just one month before the war. I wonder why the hand didn't put me in western Europe. Because I would have ended up in Paris, I suppose. If I hadn't left Europe, I would have lived in Paris after the war, that's almost certain. But the hand didn't seem to want that because, in the long run, Paris would have turned me into a Parisian. And I owed it to myself to be anti-Parisian. Now, at this period. I still wasn't sufficiently immunized. I was destined to spend many more long years on the borders of Europe, far from its capital cities, and far from the literary devices, writing, as they say in Poland today, for 'the desk drawers'. Look at the map. It would be difficult to choose a better place than Buenos Aires. The Argentine is a European country. One feels the presence of Europe there, far more forcefully than in Europe itself, yet at the same time, one is outside Europe—and besides, in that cattle country, there is no appreciation of literature. I needed that too. A distance with regard to Europe and literature.

Magic. An almost preconceived form of life. The further we move away from Form, the more we are in its power. Mysterious contradictions, contrasts . . .

We landed in Buenos Aires on 22 August (2 is my number) 1939 (the sum of the digits is also 22) after a carefree crossing which lasted three weeks. The international situation seemed to improve. But the day after our arrival the telegrams from Moscow and Berlin announcing the Nazi-Soviet pact struck the world like a thunderbolt. War! A week later the first German bombs fell on Warsaw.

I was still living on the ship with my friend Straszewicz. When he heard that war had been declared the captain decided to return to England (there was no longer any question of going back to Poland). Straszewicz and I held a war council. He opted for England. I remained in the Argentine.

In my novel *Trans-Atlantyk* I recounted these incidents and portrayed myself as a deserter. Yet there was no question of desertion, for Poland had already been cut off from the rest of the world. I presented myself at the Polish Embassy in Buenos Aires immediately after leaving the ship. Later, when a Polish army was being formed in England, I appeared naked before the recruiting commission at the Embassy. In short, on an official level, I was in order. If I pose as a deserter in *Trans-Atlantyk* it is because, morally, I was a deserter. I was distraught, in despair, but I was also glad to find myself miraculously sheltered behind the ocean.

I wrote something about my first years in the Argentine in my diary (volume 1, chapter 7). Two hundred dollars, my entire fortune, lasted me for almost six months. The Argentine was exceptionally cheap. I lived in third-class hotels. Certain Poles helped me, I started to write a bit for the newspapers—mainly serials under a pseudonym. For some time our Embassy gave me a modest grant. But that wasn't enough, I didn't know how I'd survive the next month, and I had to borrow a few pesos to eat. That continued, sometimes better, sometimes worse, according to the circumstances, until 1947, and then I worked for the next seven years in the Polish bank. It was far more boring. But the bitter, tragic, poetic taste of the first seven years had left its mark on me.

I can hardly talk about my first experiences in the Argentine—and yet I can't leave them out. I lived, as I said, in the cheapest hotels, even in what are known as the *conventillos* or doss houses. I, Mr. Gombrowicz, plunged into degradation with passion! Then, suddenly, I became young again, both morally and physically. In the street, people called me *joven*, as though I wasn't thirty-five. Never have I been so much of a poet as then, in those hot streets packed with people, completely lost (lost in the crowd, and lost, too, as far as my fate was concerned). Swarms of people, crowds, lights, a deafening din, smells, and my poverty were my joy, my fall was a new lease of life. I let myself be dragged unhesitatingly, unproblematically, into this Babel of languages. I became part of it. And my chance acquaintances, with whom I made friends with astonishing facility (I discovered this neutrality in me, in my artificial self, and it appeared as a most precious treasure, a mercy, a respite, a liberation), helped me as they could. One day, as I walked along the Calle Corrientes, I gazed longingly into the shop windows (what an honour for Mr. Gombrowicz!). I told the boy I was with that I was hungry. (What an honour!) 'Don't worry,' he said. 'I've got a corpse. There'll be enough for two.' We took a tram and rode into the suburbs, to a house in a workers' quarter where, sure enough, a dead man lay in his coffin. I don't know what nationality he was, but he was covered with flowers. And his family, friends, and acquaintances took their leave of him in macabre silence. After saying our prayers we went into the next room where a buffet had been prepared for the guests—sandwiches, wine! We ate and my friend told me that he often looked for corpses in this *barrio* and that the best way was to get the addresses from the sacristan.

This 'cadaveric' repast, this young and elegant consumption of a corpse, now seems to symbolize that period. This corpse-like feast devoured with youthful voracity, to which, at my age, I was no longer entitled. After all, my naturalness was no more than fun and games—but the most sublime, most splendid games I could play with myself. Thanks to this paradoxical taste for decomposition which I discovered in myself, I triumphantly survived war and poverty. And today I feel no remorse for having used the defeat, my misfortune or that of my family—or, indeed, that of half the world—as a bridge towards a bitter, accursed enjoyment.

No. I was entitled to do this. But I retained a certain bourgeois prudence and never let myself get involved in more dangerous exploits. The *cana* (the police) hauled me in several times, but never for very long and usually because of my friends rather than because of any crime I had committed.

And here's another recollection, which also seems symbolic to me: in March 1942, the owner of my hotel started insisting far too energetically on the six months arrears I owed him, so I had to move out. One night I left the hotel and my neighbour, Don Alfredo, magnanimously passed me my bags through the window. I took them to a café, sat at a table, and didn't know what to do. My credit had run out. Suddenly I heard: 'You here?' It was a Pole, a journalist named Taworski, who had lived in the Argentine for many years.

I told him what had happened. 'You know,' he replied, 'I now have some partners and we've rented a villa near Buenos Aires, at Moron, in order to set up a small textile industry. You can live there.' The villa wasn't bad—five rooms overlooking a garden, admittedly completely unfurnished. Taworski slept on a bed and I on a heap of newspapers. From the moment I arrived, he warned me mysteriously: 'If someone comes in, even through the window, even at night, for God's sake don't budge. Don't betray any sign of life.'

I spent a few peaceful nights on my heap of newspapers. Then, one night, at about three in the morning, some noises woke me up, and I saw two huge fellows who were unscrewing the light bulbs and removing the fuses. I didn't move. They disappeared. It turned out that they were Taworski's partners who couldn't get their own back on him or throw him out and who played every trick they could on him. Taworski himself had already been given a suspended prison sentence for some little prank and didn't dare protest—and they knew it. So these brutal, nightly, drunken, (because they were usually drunk) visits, together with our inability to defend ourselves, took on the quality of a symbol, as pathetic as it was significant.

I spent about six months in this villa, which was gradually being stripped. Taworski was goodness itself and looked after me like a father. We lived almost exclusively on smoked meat and maize which he cooked once a week. I was very popular at Moron, both at the pizzeria in the square and at the café where I played billiards and chess. I drank my daily pint of milk and ate my bread in the sun, sitting on the grass, looking at the street. At the pizzeria a *mozo* who had taken a liking to me gave me a sandwich costing twenty centos with a slice of ham in it four times thicker than usual—it was almost a beefsteak.

And then suddenly, in a literary supplement of *La Nación*, an article by me appeared on the front page. After that my social position at Moron was liquidated. People started treating me with consideration.

Life was not easy. I was sustained by catastrophe. My catastrophe, Poland's catastrophe, Europe's catastrophe. But at the same time I acted on another, more elevated level.

I didn't have much to do with the literary circles in the Argentine. To begin with I made an effort to establish contact with them for practical purposes. But I soon gave up. To start with because my books weren't translated into any language and were quite inaccessible to them. Then because, during my first years in the Argentine, my Spanish was appalling. And finally because I wasn't conventional enough for them. If I had been able to engage in conversations on the 'new literary values' in Poland or France, or on 'Mallarmé's influence on Valéry' I might have had more luck.

As for Victoria Ocampo, [*] I don't want to repeat what I've already written in my diary. If I managed to enjoy a certain fame in the Argentine it was not as an author, but as the one and only foreign writer who had not made a pilgrimage to Señora Ocampo's salon. I was convinced that my opinions, my behaviour, and my work would be too shocking for her. As far as my books were concerned, the appearance of *Ferdydurke* in the Argentine confirmed my suspicions, because the review *Sur*, which she edited, was the only magazine not to mention it.

Borges and I are at opposite poles. He is deeply rooted in literature, I in life. To tell the truth I am anti-literature. Precisely because of that, a meeting with Borges might have proved fruitful, but technical difficulties intervened. We met once or twice, but we left it at that. Borges already had his rather too obsequious little court. He spoke and they listened.

What he said didn't seem to me of any great value. It was too narrow, too literary, paradoxes, witticisms, subtleties—in short, the sort of thing I hate. His intelligence did not stagger me. It was only later, when I read his really artistic works, his stories, that I had to admit that he had an exceptional intellectual perspicacity. But the 'spoken' Borges, the Borges

---

[*] Victoria Ocampo, a formidable literary personality in the Argentine, is best known for her foundation of the literary magazine, and publishing house, *Sur*.

of conversations, lectures, interviews, and also of essays and literary criticism, always seemed to me somewhat superficial. In the Argentine, I often heard his 'brilliant' *bons mots* quoted. Well, each time I was disappointed. It was nothing but literature, and not of the best.

I have a theory of my own about this striking difference between Borges' art and the spoken Borges. To my mind, not enough importance has been attached to the fact that Borges is almost blind. This is what enabled him to develop those formidable powers of concentration which gave birth to works of art of great value. But this is also what forced him to live in a narrow circle formed by men of letters, none of whom was of sufficient calibre to contradict him. He was force-fed on this rather fragile admiration, he was followed ever further along the fine arabesques of his thoughts and of his pseudo-erudition (all erudition is, and can only be, pseudo; Borges' erudition stems from an abysmal ignorance and he himself is of a questionable intelligence, because erudition is essentially unintelligent). Consequently, in his blindness, Borges became increasingly profound and, in his dealings with the outer world, increasingly superficial. Such a development deserves respect, since a blind man is not in a condition to lead a normal life. But I believe that his admirers are mistaken in not distinguishing between the two Borges and in enveloping his intelligence and his lack of intelligence in the same cloud of incense—a lack of intelligence which manifests itself as much in the maniacal picking at worthless literary crumbs as in a revelation such as this: 'What do you think of duelling?' 'I'm dead against it. If two people disagree about something, I don't see that this disagreement has anything to do with swords or with anybody's death.'

One might object to this. If the fact that Borges is limited or intellectually eccentric is due to his blindness, you could say, he wouldn't have been like that when his sight was still good enough. And yet, when he started writing, Borges was less original and still more imprisoned by his aestheticism, both in what he wrote and in what he said. This is true, of course. So perhaps we should say that blindness did not allow him to triumph in everyday life, as a wit and as a critic, though it enabled him to triumph in his art. I don't know.

I have been hard on his art. In one chapter of my diary, I described it as an 'insipid soup for men of letters'. I expressed myself badly. For I respect him greatly as an artist. But he has such an irritating knack of attracting aesthetes, scholars, 'chisellers', bibliophiles, professors, commentators, and other sybarites and specialists in literature! It was they whom I meant by 'insipid soup', not Borges.

In the Argentine, I had the opportunity of meeting some of those members of his inner circle. They didn't strike me by their excessive intelligence or by their excessive intellectual energy. There is nothing surprising in the fact that they didn't understand a single word of *Ferdydurke*, which had just been translated into Spanish. But even if Borges' acolytes had proved capable of giving him a vague idea about it (to him who is incapable of reading on his own), it wouldn't have been of any use. This man, who is very sincere and profoundly humane in his solitude, is frightened of men in daily life. His shyness, his aristocratic finesse, make him run away from sincerity. His so-called modesty is nothing but a shield for his aristocratic arrogance. Modest Sir Jorge Borges, Knight of the British Empire, Commandeur des Lettres et des Arts, Caballero de la Orden del Sol, Caballero de la Orden de la Madonnina, etc., would have, I feel, great difficulty in seeing eye to eye with a vain man called Gombrowicz.

I hardly had any dealings with the other Argentinian writers. One could only speak of dealings after the publication of *Ferdydurke*, and by then I already had seven years of the Argentine behind me. But by that time I had become accustomed to my anonymity and I didn't give a damn about the literary world. I was free, independent, capricious, provocative. I was used to the fact that nobody took me seriously and that I took nobody seriously. Besides, a work like *Ferdydurke* needed the blessing of Paris for them to be able to recognize me!

Together with the group of young writers who collaborated in the translation, I had launched this powerful pamphlet in a rather frivolous atmosphere. *Ferdydurke* found a number of enthusiasts, mainly among the young. A good many reviews appeared in the papers, but it all fizzled out. It was at this moment that I started my job at the Banco Polaco and so the last reason I might have had for getting in touch with Argentinian literature, that is to say the prospect of scraping a few coins together, vanished.

I was told that not long ago an attaché at the Argentinian Embassy in Paris told an attaché at the Polish Embassy: 'Gombrowicz ate our bread for a quarter of a century and now he's slandering our country.' I'm not slandering the Argentine—at the most I may make a few slightly slanderous remarks about the Argentinian bourgeoisie, but that's not the same thing. Besides, my Argentinian bread came from abroad. To start with, the Poles helped me a little, and then the Banco Polaco paid me, and finally I lived on what I earned from foreign publications of my works. Only once, if I remember rightly, did an Argentinian writer, a millionaire, promise to leave me three hundred pesos in an envelope which would enable me to convalesce in Cordoba, in the mountains, and recover from an attack of 'flu. He left the envelope, but I only found one hundred and fifty pesos in it.

Things didn't change very much when I was discovered in Europe either. At first people thought it was a false rumour. A year before I left the Argentine—about five years after *Ferdydurke* had been published in Paris—at a time when I was being translated into most European languages, I came across the poet Jorge Calvetti in the street. I told him about my success and Calvetti, who wrote for the best paper in the country, *La Prensa*, did a two column interview with me. But then another man who wrote for the same paper, a friend of Borges called Manuel Peyrou, met Calvetti at the paper's offices and attacked him violently for having been taken in by my lies. There was a terrible row. Calvetti complained to the editor. Fortunately a well-known critic from Paris, the Russian Wladimir Weidlé, whose books had a great success in the Argentine, happened to be passing through Buenos Aires. The editor told Calvetti to check his facts with him, and Weidlé settled the matter by confirming that I was a well-known and much appreciated writer in Europe, and *La Prensa* proclaimed this. Apparently Calvetti and Peyrou were so cross with each other that one of them had to be immobilized in a lift between two floors to stop them from coming to blows. *Se non è vero. . . .*

But what could they care about a foreigner who had admittedly lived a long time in their country, but whom they never saw, never met at their tea parties, their dinners, their banquets—even though that foreigner had acquired a certain notoriety? No nation can benefit from me, a permanently private individual. I am an outsider. In the international match I was never a member of their literary team.

I should add, however, that I did indeed meet kind and helpful people. Virgilio Piniera, a Cuban writer who is now famous, and Humberto Rodríguez Tomeu, another Cuban, did a great deal for me. It is above all to them that I owe the Spanish translation of *Ferdydurke*. Cecilia Debenedetti, Alejandro Russovich, Jorge Calvetti, Adolfo de Obieta, Roger Pla, these are some of the names which are inscribed in my memory.

My friendship with Ernesto Sabato originated much later, when I was fascinated by his great novel *Sobre hèroes y tumbas (Alexander)*, a really extraordinary work in which romanticism, tradition, history, a sort of telluric anachronism, and obscure South American pathology combine in a strange manner with an *avant-garde* modernism which expresses contemporary Argentine. Sabato is undoubtedly one of the three 'greats' of Latin America, together with Asturias and Borges.

Throughout the war I only wrote short features for the newspapers under a pseudonym, in order to earn some money, and a few articles for *La Nación.* It was impossible to write because I didn't know where my next penny was coming from. From time to time, in short periods of remission, I planned my play, *The Marriage*, but I didn't finish it until after the war.

The war. It was a holiday, a holiday which had its moments of ghastly depression in the loneliness and humiliation beyond the ocean, when my black humour deserted me. Yes, I suppose it was painful, terrible, desperate. The war destroyed my family, my social position, my country, my future. I had nothing left, and I was nobody. And yet! And yet. And yet, the Argentine. What a relief! What a liberation! When I think of my first and hardest years in the Argentine the words of Mickiewicz come to mind:

> *Born in bonds, mapped in my swaddling clothes,*
> *I only knew one such spring in my life!*

Mickiewicz was referring to 1812, when Napoleon marched on Russia and liberated Poland for a brief period, while I apply these words to the time of Poland's collapse, the outbreak of war, to the time when everything crashed about me—the entire order I had hitherto lived in. . . .

The accepted forms of life had collapsed!

An exceptional opportunity! A unique and blessed occasion! You see, those who took part in the war immediately found themselves gripped by new expressions of Form, which were even more rigid than before—the army, service, action. Whereas the war plunged *me* into billows of noise and dizziness, instants with no future, stretching almost to nothingness. Alone. Liberated. Lost.

I knew it well. It was an opportunity presented to me by fate so that I could at last approach what was most sacred for me, something I defined as 'inferiority', 'degradation', or 'lowness', or 'freshness', 'simplicity', 'immaturity', or even as an 'obscure and unmentionable element'—these words do not even approximately convey the nature of this secret, of this goal which my books could neither really reveal or express. In all events I found myself two steps from the high altar of this inaccessible church—and I flung myself into the whirlpool like a man dying of thirst! No, to tell the truth it was neither a holiday nor a period of relaxation. If poverty, humiliation, war, defeat, loneliness, insecurity, shoes full of holes, cold, fleas, a thousand pains and worries, if all this is reduced to almost nothing, it is because I had never felt so close to beauty, to a certain unique beauty—and I then abandoned myself to this mad hope that I could appropriate this beauty, that this beauty would be mine.

Yes, I who am fairly lucid, I was obsessed for weeks on end by this poetic intoxication, to the point of feeling myself to be poetry!

Mirages. No, it wasn't a holiday, but a painful and exhausting ordeal. Because, in order to approach simplicity and naturalness, I had to don masks, and it was a trick, a sleight of hand, it grated, it sounded hollow, I repeat, I didn't get anywhere in the end, I only got closer. And getting closer emphasized my falseness! Miserable buffoon! When I was almost forty I led the life of a man of twenty, and I relived that age—during the Holocaust—and that alone sufficed to show how reckless my undertaking was.

I don't know. The demands of our ego are indomitable, they are so powerful that I was sometimes led to believe that this world catastrophe was only intended to put me in the Argentine and plunge me into the youth which I hadn't been able to experience or exploit at the time. That was why the war broke out, that was the reason for the Argentine and Buenos Aires.

7

THE MARRIAGE AND *TRANS-ATLANTYK*

I shall only say a few words about *The Marriage* and *Trans-Atlantyk*, not because I accord them a second place but because *Ferdydurke*, my diary, and *Pornografia* are probably a better introduction to my life.

I had started *The Marriage* during the war. It gradually grew inside me, in fits and starts, during my stay in the Argentine, day by day. *Faust* and *Hamlet* were my models, but only because of their quality of genius. I wanted to write a 'great' play, a 'work of genius', and I went back to those works which I had read with veneration in my youth. And my ambitions were accompanied by a certain cunning. I sensed slyly that it was easier to write a 'great' work than simply a 'good' work. The paths of genius seemed less arduous to me.

Why? *The Marriage* which, like all my works, rebels against Form, is a parody of Form, a parody of a play of genius. But by parodying genius, was I not going to sneak a little of my own genius into the parody—to smuggle it in?

I wanted to show humanity in its transition from the church of God to the church of man. Yet this idea was not contained in the work from the start. I started by casting a handful of visions onto the stage, germs, situations, and gradually, somehow, I arrived at this idea. When I reached the middle of the second act I still didn't know what I wanted. And the stumbling, drunken, or somnambulistic development of my *Missa Solemnis* out of a series of short circuits of Form, of connections and combinations, of rhymes and inner rhythms, seemed to correspond to the development of history, which also advances in a drunken, somnabulistic state.

When I wrote:

Johnny: Nothing.
Henry: Nothing.
The father: Transformed.
The mother: Dislocated.
Johnny: Overthrown.
Henry: Distorted.

I suddenly burst into tears like a child. Nothing like this has ever happened to me before or since—my nerves, of course!

I wept bitterly and my tears ran onto the paper. What filled me with such despair was not so much the fact that these words evoked a personal catastrophe, as the fact that they came to me so easily. I felt their rhythm and their rhyme like a relentless thorn. I wept with horror at the internal coherence of misfortune. Then I stopped weeping and started writing again.

I translated *The Marriage* into Spanish with the assistance of my friend Alexander Russovich and, thanks to Cecilia Debenedetti and Stanislas Odyniec, it was published in

Buenos Aires. The artistic circles in the capital hardly noticed it. In 1963, Jorge Lavelli, a young Argentinian director living in Paris, took an interest in it. He staged it at the Theatre Recamier and his excellent production launched him on a successful career. *The Marriage* was later produced by a great director, Alf Sjoberg, at the Royal Dramatic Theatre of Stockholm. Sjoberg put a great deal of work and passion into the rehearsals of *The Marriage* and then of *Princess Ivona*, and the two plays had a tremendous success. The third of the best productions of *The Marriage* was at the Schiller Theater in Berlin, where there were fifty-one curtain calls on the first night. I owe that to the director Ernst Schroder and a troupe of excellent actors, above all to Helmut Greim. Unfortunately, by a concurrence of annoying circumstances, I didn't see any of these performances. To tell the truth I haven't set foot in a theatre for at least thirty years. I write plays, but I never go to any . . . I don't know why . . . out of laziness, perhaps.

I don't compare my plays with Beckett or Ionesco: it's the critics who do that. When *Princess Ivona* and *The Marriage* were produced in Paris they wrote that it was 'theatre of the absurd', like Beckett and Ionesco. But *Princess Ivona* was written in 1936 and *The Marriage* in 1946, when nobody had heard of either of these writers. Besides, my plays are not absurd.

Yes, *The Marriage* is obscure, somnambulistic, extravagant. I myself am unable to decipher it entirely; so much of it is in the dark. And the director who left that kind of sphinx free to choose its own form, to shout and to rave, was right: he himself only saw to the almost musical harmonization of the ceremony. Nevertheless, *The Marriage* does have a plot which stands up on its own and there is no reason why it should not be perceptible to the spectators. In a way, I would like these pages to constitute a sort of clue to my work, so I shall tell the story of *The Marriage*. It might be useful to some director.

What The Marriage *is about*. It is a dream, dreamt by Henry, a Polish soldier in the last war, who finds himself somewhere in France, in the French army, fighting the Germans. Within this dream Henry's concern for his family, lost in Poland, emerges together with the more essential worries of contemporary man straddling the slopes of two epochs.

In his dream Henry sees the house where he was born in Poland, his parents, his fiancée, Molly. The house has gone to seed. It has now been transformed into an inn: Molly is a serving maid working at the inn, and the father is the innkeeper.

The father is pursued by drunkards. This is the key scene. In order to defend his human dignity before the drunkards' onslaught he claims that he is 'untouchable'.

'Untouchable—like a king!' laugh the drunkards.

And Henry pays homage to his father, while his father becomes king. And not only does the father-king elevate Henry to the rank of prince but he also promises him, by virtue of his royal power, a worthy religious marriage which will restore the purity and former integrity of Molly, the maidservant.

With that, the first act ends. Human dignity, one might say, has been saved.

In the second act we see the preparations for this worthy and religious marriage which must be celebrated by a bishop. But doubts begin to pervade Henry's dream. This whole marriage ceremony begins to vacillate, as if threatened by stupidity—as if Henry, aspiring with all his soul to goodness, dignity, purity, lacked confidence in himself and his dream.

The drunkard-in-chief again enters the room, as tight as a tick! Henry is about to come to blows with him when suddenly (as happens in dreams) the scene changes into a court banquet. The drunkard has become the ambassador of a hostile power. He incites Henry to treason.

'Betray your father the king,' is more or less what the drunkard tells him, 'the Bishop, the King, the Church, God, are nothing but antiquated superstitions. Proclaim yourself king and then no authority, divine or otherwise, will be necessary. You'll bestow on yourself the sacrament of matrimony and you'll oblige everybody to recognize it and to recognize Molly as pure and united with you.'

This is the key to the metaphor of *The Marriage,* the transition of a world based on divine authority, divine and paternal authority, to another world, where Henry's own will must become the divine, creative will . . . like the will of Hitler or Stalin.

Henry yields to the drunkard's insistence. He deposes the father-king and becomes ruler himself.

A scene follows in which the drunkard asks Johnny, Henry's friend, to hold a flower over Molly's head. Then he suddenly conjures away the flower, leaving them in a false position which no flower can justify. And a ghastly conjecture forms in Henry's mind that Molly and Johnny. . . .

'Priest-pig, you have bound them in a base and ignoble marriage!' he exclaims.

End of act two.

In the third act, Henry is dictator. He has dominated the whole world, including his parents. And once again the marriage ceremony is prepared, but it is a marriage without God, with no sanction other than that of Henry's absolute power.

But he feels that his power will have no real validity as long as it is not confirmed by someone who voluntarily sacrifices his blood. That is why he urges Johnny to volunteer to kill himself for him. This sacrifice will both appease his jealousy and make him powerful and formidable enough to perform the marriage . . . and reassert Molly's purity (as well as to make the dream come true . . . which is his purpose from the start). Johnny agrees.

In the last scene Johnny kills himself. But Henry steps back. He recoils, horrified by his act.

The marriage will not take place.

This is the story. It tries to express the anxiety and the terrors of the man faced by the world to come, where he will be both his own God and his own king. Henry's apotheosis comes about through the domination of others, like Hitler's apotheosis.

In *The Marriage* one can find some of the mechanisms which generate modern man and modern humanity. The constant presence of Form on the stage is the moving spirit of the play.

Something is said, and then we adapt ourselves to what has been said. One word creates another. One scene, another one. The continual necessity of organizing reality in a rational structure is illuminated by the dramatic development on the stage.

Once one lets oneself be dragged into the whirlwinds of Form which is being constantly and consciously created one is for ever imprisoned in this mortal doubt: does it really exist? Is it cleverness? Or stupidity? Reality or dream?

Trans-Atlantyk is not a ship: it is something more like 'across the Atlantic', it's a novel directed towards Poland from the Argentine.

It always amuses me, this facetious, sclerotic, baroque, absurd *Trans-Atlantyk*, written in an archaic style, full of idiomatic jokes and inventions.

It is the least known of my novels because these linguistic eccentricities are not easy to translate. I shall talk about it briefly.

The end of the war did not bring liberty to the Poles. In that sad area of central Europe, it was merely a question of exchanging Hitler's executioners for Stalin's. At a time when high-minded liberals, seated in Parisian cafés, greeted 'the emancipation of the Polish people from the feudal yoke' with a joyous anthem, in Poland the same lighted cigarette simply changed hands and continued to burn the human skin. I watched all that from the Argentine, walking along the Avenida Costanera. The word 'enough', which was surely on the lips of every Pole, began to demand a concrete solution. If Poland saw itself condemned to being eternally torn on account of its geographical position and its history, was it not possible for us Poles to change something within ourselves, to rescue our humanity?

Besides their brutality, another aspect of these facts tormented me . . . a falsity accompanied it all, some interplay of forces, a plot . . . One of the mysteries of Form is that one doesn't know either how or why a certain way of acting artificially, falsely, conventionally, accompanied by a certain perfectly unbearable phraseology, is created before certain phenomena, certain people, certain nations. As long as people were having their teeth knocked out in Poland, the world would continue to expatiate on 'Polish romanticism' and 'Polish idealism', or repeat the same clichés about 'martyred Poland'. Or we would be discussed reluctantly, condescendingly, pityingly. In the cinemas of Buenos Aires I saw the Poles charge on their white horses, their eyes blazing. So it wasn't enough for people to get punched over there. To make matters worse the great civilized world was going to poke fun at their bruised faces.

And that seemed to me still more dangerous than the defeat and the pain themselves: it was a disquieting symptom. Just as you say that someone or other had bad reviews, you can say that Poland had 'bad poetry'. (And how many times, subsequently, did I not read, in articles about me in European or American papers, these same clichés from which, being a Pole, I could never escape? It was as though it were impossible to talk about us normally.)

Whose fault was it? That of a certain anachronism peculiar to the Polish character? That of the intellectual idleness of the West, which shows a marked preference for worn-out formulas? Our relationship with the world had something bad, something tainted about it, and I, as an artist, felt somewhat responsible for this fateful 'Polish legend'. It was essential to put an end to it. But how?

As far as art is concerned I don't believe in the use of minor corrections, little patches, careful alterations. One must summon up one's strength and leap, implement a radical, fundamental change. But which? Sunk in chimeras, illusions, phraseology, the Poles were at the same time very close to crude reality, to reality unadorned by phrases, to that reality which breaks your bones. It was a trump to play. Only the most merciless realism could rescue us from the morass of our 'legend'. I believe in the purifying power of reality.

We needed more than a second-hand reality, a Polish reality, we needed the most fundamental, and most human, sense of reality. The Pole had to be removed from Poland and simply turned into a man. In other words, the Pole had to be made an anti-Pole.

This idea wasn't new to me. I had already had something similar in mind when writing *Ferdydurke*—it was always the same idea. Beware of Form. In this case, of national form.

Was this idea out of place, inadmissible in the circumstances in which we found ourselves, at the depths of the catastrophe? Was it presuming upon the possibilities of the Polish intellectual elite (or of any national elite) to propose such a programme? I didn't take any notice of all this. Once it has been expressed the most savage thought civilises itself a hundred times faster than one can imagine. I knew that the Pole was ripe for change, that he'd had enough, that he no longer wanted to be as he was, that he wanted to be different. I knew this for sure, despite what all those Poles could say about themselves, in their language inherited from the past. That was enough for me.

And there was something else. My programme does not precede my work. On the contrary, it always appears *post factum* . . . I simply sat down and started writing . . . and I wrote. . . . But then I wrote something completely opposed to what I should have written. Instead of something serious—laughter, idiocies, somersaults, fun!

Sublimation in reverse. What could the reasons for this tragic spirit of contradiction be? One can sometimes conceal provocation in an apparently innocent game. But here quite the opposite occurred. It was precisely this playful quality in *Trans-Atlantyk* which constituted its greatest provocation. Like a burst of laughter at a funeral. Very indecent, isn't it? It even surprises me. At the darkest hour of our history, when we would have done better to sing a Requiem mass. But what if that was the expression of my national pride? Another contradiction. Some of my compatriots regard me as an exceptionally Polish author—and I may well be both very anti-Polish and very Polish—or perhaps Polish because anti-Polish; because the Pole comes to life in me spontaneously, freely, to the extent in which he becomes stronger than I (that's how far I had got since *Ferdydurke*).

I wouldn't be at all surprised if the black humour of *Trans-Atlantyk* were an almost involuntary expression of Polish pride and liberty.

And . . . you know how much I fear every kind of teaching, of spiritual authority . . . I don't want to teach like a professor, I want my life and work to be a lesson, I want to be a lesson *myself*.

So, to start with, this 'programme' manifested itself in my tone, my style, a bold laugh in the face of tragedy. It appeared in my unceremonious treatment of sacrosanct Polish traditions. Literature is not a Sunday School, it is the verbal expression of the *fait accompli*. Someone who begins to talk about something differently—that's important.

Listen, this is how I cursed Poland:

> Drift, drift towards your country! Your holy and accursed country! Drift towards that Obscure Monstrous-Saint who has been dying for centuries but cannot give up! Drift towards this holy crank, cursed by nature, for ever being born, newborn for ever. Drift, drift, so that he will neither let you live nor die, and will keep you suspended for ever between Being and Not-Being! Drift towards your Raving Lunatic . . . so that his lunacy can torture you, your wife and your children, so that he can condemn and assassinate you in his agony, by his agony!

You could get beaten up for something like that. And, as I left the Banco Polaco after work, I glanced round discreetly because the Polish colony in Buenos Aires was large and quick on the draw.

Nobody beat me up. My curse was decked in a buffoon's livery, thanks to which I could smuggle in a fair quantity of dynamite.

Trans-Atlantyk was such folly, from every point of view! To think that I wrote something like that, just when I was isolated on the American continent, without a penny, deserted by God and men! In my position, it was important to write something quickly which could be translated and published in foreign languages. Or, if I wanted to write something for the Poles, something which didn't injure their national pride. And I dared—the very height of irresponsibility!—to fabricate a novel which was inaccessible to foreigners because of its linguistic difficulties and which was a deliberate provocation of the Polish émigrés, the only readership on which I could rely!

That is what happens in the hour of defeat. One writes, in spite of everything, for one's own pleasure. What a luxury I permitted myself in my misery!

Nevertheless, the novel was published in Polish. This was very laudable of *Kultura*, the monthly review that printed it in Paris. Precautions were taken. Jozef Wittlin, an excellent writer who commanded great authority amongst the émigrés, agreed to write a preface and, under the wing of his prestige, *Trans-Atlantyk* sailed onto the sea of Polish literature. People ignored it. It was too bizarre to be taken seriously. The dynamite passed unnoticed.

The plot of *Trans-Atlantyk*? For me, plots are never very important, they are only a pretext. In an archaic prose, as though it were set in the distant past, I tell how, just before the war, I landed in the Argentine, how war broke out when I was there.

I, Gombrowicz, make the acquaintance of a *puto* (a queer) who is in love with a young Pole, and circumstances make me arbiter of the situation: I can throw the young man into the queer's arms or make him stay with his father, a very honourable, dignified, and old-fashioned Polish major.

To throw him into the *puto's* arms is to deliver him up to vice, to set him on roads which lead nowhere, into the troubled waters of the abnormal, of limitless liberty, of an uncontrollable future.

To wrench him away from the queer and make him return to his father is to keep him within the confines of the honest Polish tradition.

What should I choose? Fidelity to the past . . . or the freedom to create oneself as one will? Shut him into his atavistic form . . . or open the cage, let him fly away and do what he likes! Let him create himself! In the novel, the dilemma leads up to a general burst of laughter, which sweeps away the dilemma.

And another confession. I have already told you that when I wrote *The Marriage* I was influenced by *Hamlet* and *Faust*. Well, in a sense *Trans-Atlantyk* was born in me like a *Pan Tadeusz* in reverse. This epic poem, written by Mickiewicz in exile over a hundred years ago, the masterpiece of Polish poetry, is an assertion of the Polish spirit inspired by nostalgia. In *Trans-Atlantyk*, I wanted to do the opposite to Mickiewicz. As you see, I always make sure that I am in the best possible company!

8

THE DIARY

In 1952, I was working as a secretary at the Banco Polaco in Buenos Aires. I was a pitiful secretary! I worked for a starvation wage, about a hundred dollars a month, and I had no outlets for making extra money. An eminent anti-talent in banking matters, I understood nothing about all those documents: the hours went by, absurd, exasperating, sterile . . . I tried to write *Trans-Atlantyk* and when the manager came in I stuffed my papers into a drawer like a schoolboy.

It was at that moment—as I said—that I started writing for *Kultura*, the main Polish emigre review, printed in Paris. For the first time in fifteen years, I publicly expressed myself in Polish. I presented my second or third piece in diary form. 'This medium suits you,' the editor, Jerzy Giedroyc, wrote to me. 'Maybe you should continue with it.'

From then, right up to this very day, I have written my diary for *Kultura*. Three volumes, a thousand pages, have appeared, and a fourth volume is in preparation. I hardly ever write any articles or essays. All I can say outside pure art is crammed into my diary.

Although it is banned in Poland many people read it there, above all among the young. It is read more than any of my other works. But only in Poland. *Ferdydurke*, *Pornografia*, and *Cosmos* have already appeared in about fifteen countries. The first volume of my diary, on the other hand, has only been published in French, German, and Dutch. It will soon be appearing in the United States, the Argentine, and Italy. The other volumes haven't yet been translated.

I don't know why the diary arouses less interest. Some people believe that these aggressive notes reveal me and my work in a different light, in addition to constituting a very personal view of culture. The papers emphasized this, and one critic said it was thought that every taboo had been abolished, and yet my diary uncovers whole areas of culture hitherto untouched by criticism.

People buy a diary because the author is famous, while I wrote mine in order to become famous. That is where the misunderstanding lies.

And then me . . . with my life! If one removed the collection of famous names from Gide's diaries, I should imagine that he would lose a number of his readers. Where are my meetings with d'Annunzio or my conversations with Claudel? I described myself at the Cafe Rex with my friend Eisler, winning a few pennies from him whenever I beat him at chess. My life was uneventful. If my diary had not come about on its own, imperceptibly, month after month, I would never have felt able to tackle it. A diary? Me? With my life? What an idea!

Nor is the fact that I led a double, triple, quadruple life in Poland and the Argentine particularly interesting. It's too complicated, too far out of reach. And my secret life did not have that force and colour which are the material of the memoirs of true vagabonds. I would have had to invent things, to rearrange them. So what could I fill this diary with? Intellectual delicacies . . . let's say with comparisons between St. John of the Cross and Erasmus of Rotterdam? Political titbits? Not even that. An empty shop, nothing to offer.

Only, as I told you, it started little by little, month by month. And that is why I consider literature non-heroic. Everything in it takes place imperceptibly, and even the higher obstacles ultimately disappear.

Ah! I forgot another difficulty. For the artist who has acquired a relatively sure touch in a given medium—lyrical, epic, grotesque, let us say—it is very dangerous to change rails, to pass on to another mode of expression. And the transition from the language of art to ordinary prose can turn into a disaster: such a manoeuvre engages the writer's entire personality. I was afraid of that! Release the metaphors, the style, write normally? I already had twenty years of literary work behind me and I was as scared as a beginner.

Yet I needed all this.

I had already written a dozen short stories, two plays, and a novel. And if, to start with, I had some hope of gradually becoming more accessible, more intelligible, it had now become obvious that people still didn't know what to look for in me, how to come to grips with me. Who could make me accessible, explain me? The critics? Sooner or later, every writer not only realizes that criticism will never be of any use to him, but that it is an additional obstacle between him and the reader. It is a most depressing discovery. The work of art aspires to originality, and even the best form of criticism catalogues, classifies, levels you, melts you down, makes a mass product of you. This is contrary to the very essence of art, which is why it is so unpleasant, and sounds so false. And so far nobody has found a way of preventing Mr. X from sounding arrogant and sententious when he writes a little article on Homer—that's irritating, too. I don't believe there is a single artist who does not end up by understanding that the critic is an enemy, even when he covers him with flowers.

Down there, in the Argentine, on the banks of a vast and sleepy river, I was oppressed by an infinite loneliness. Unfortunately, today art becomes more and more difficult. I was difficult myself. Even in *Ferdydurke*, in order to facilitate things for the reader, I had assumed the role of a commentator. Only my commentaries were inadequate. Well, in more favourable conditions, had I lived in Saint-Gennain-des-Près and frequented the Café des Deux Magots, my works would have waged a hard battle. But I was an *avant-garde* writer, an innovator, an outsider moreover, and I felt increasingly crushed by the weight of war, revolution, exile, and twenty million Argentinian cows. What should I do? What could I do? In such a situation how could the subtle commentaries and interpretations aimed at a distinguished elite suffice? No, I knew it, nobody would take any interest in me until I had extricated myself from the enclosure of art, until I had resorted to my normal voice and introduced people to my everyday existence. The Parisian innovators could allow themselves the luxury of an ivory tower, but I couldn't. Nothing isolated *me* from the street, or the crowd. *I* did not have a salon.

Even as I wrote *Ferdydurke*, my main concern had been to combine art with my own real situation, to fight for myself, to impose myself. But this time I tackled the matter in a different way. It happened just like that, almost unintentionally. And it took me still longer to notice that my serialized diary started to take the form of a polemic with the world.

This serial, published in *Kultura*, a Parisian-Polish monthly review, aroused the protests of the readers, but I didn't care, they were usually too primitive. After two years I had to look the whole thing over with an eye to having it published in one volume. I wondered if I should write a preface. Instead of that I wrote, as a foreword:

Monday: myself
Tuesday: myself
Wednesday: myself
Thursday: myself.

And I found myself in sharp conflict with all the post-war tendencies which condemned the word 'myself'. This 'myself' was excommunicated by the Church as being immoral, it was frowned upon by Science as being in contradiction with objectivism, it was banned by Marxism and by every current of the time which wanted man to despise his selfish, egocentric, old-fashioned, antisocial, 'self'. Severe admonishments came from all sides: you are nothing, forget yourself, live through others! When I wrote 'myself' for the fourth time, I felt like Antaeus as he touched the earth! I felt the ground under my feet once more!

To assert myself in this 'myself', in spite of everything,

with the maximum insolence, with a certain stubborn non-chalance, in an unexaggerated, quite natural manner—this, I realized, was the purpose of my diary. Starting, of course, with my own needs and my most personal imperatives.

That is to say that I had to start by obtaining the right to speak.

For, according to contemporary convention, the artist can only express himself partially. He can 'sing', but he is not entitled to talk. He has to turn his face towards art, not towards men. It would be too tactless if this priest who was saying mass at the altar suddenly cared what people were doing with him, behind him, and if, for example, he decided to draw his sword in order to defend such and such an interpretation of his work and of his person (one thing entails another). So the artist is virtually unarmed.

Pride? Am I proud? It is the most natural right of self-defence in the world. What pride? It's the very opposite. If there is such a thing as a 'proud' view it is what I would call the 'aseptic-aristocratic' view, according to which the artist-priest cannot 'lower himself', and has to pretend to be inaccessible to other people's judgement. What I call the 'aristocratic-socialist' view is also proud. It gives the artist the right and even the obligation to face men, but only as a pedagogue, a guide, a spiritual nurse, in a word, as a superior being. Do you know the basic reason for the artist's inability to descend from his pedestal? It is this: he cannot admit that he is fighting for his own superiority. He 'sings'. But he sings in order to rise. So, fie! Fie!

Nevertheless every work of art possesses two faces. It is disinterested. It is composed of pure contemplation, but it is also the result of an ambition, of a desire to be superior to others. The artist craves for approval. And even if he is as disinterested and as pure as a tear, this purity still contributes to the success of his work. It is the path to personal expansion! To pass over this second aspect of art in silence is to impoverish it, to falsify it, and . . . and . . . Oh, hell! Should I, the author, let every man disfigure me as he likes?

I had already fought for this in *Ferdydurke*: I had demanded the right to show my own face. But in my diary I discovered the potential of everyday language. What wasn't particularly shocking in *Ferdydurke* became almost indecent when said in a matter-of-fact way in my diary. What! A virtually unknown little writer who won't hold his tongue or wait for others to praise him, but who insists on advertising himself?! Who shouts himself hoarse so that everyone will know his opinions and his private tastes! As if people were interested! What's going on? Self-publicity? Delusions of grandeur? Or is the reader being made fun of?

Some of my colleagues, émigré Polish writers, were ready to accuse me of unsporting competition. Now that I'm an established writer, my diary is no longer so shocking. But at the time it was infuriating. I touched on the most important aspect of morality: convention. My pride was all the more intolerable since it came to me so easily.

Yet such pride can only really hail from exceptional modesty. He who says, 'I want to be great' is infinitely less attached to himself, treats himself with greater objectivity, than the man who blushes at the mere thought of such a confession. He is more objective, he admits his subjectivity.

You may think that my method is 'confession'—a confes-

sion of immaturity or of a desire for superiority and maturity—sincerity, self-revelation. But this is far from being
the case. Literature wriggles away like an eel. What would
become of the eel if you caught it? You'd eat it. Literature
and the eel live as long as they succeed in wriggling away.

Sincerity?

As a writer, it is what I fear most. In literature, sincerity leads
nowhere. There is another of the dynamic antinomies of art:
the more artificial we are, the closer we come to frankness.
Artificiality allows the artist to approach shameful truths. As
for my diary . . . have you ever read a 'sincere' diary? The
'sincere' diary is the most mendacious diary, because sincerity
is not of this world. And, in the long run, what a bore sincerity is! It is ineffectual!

Then what? My diary had to be sincere, but it could not
be sincere. How could I solve the problem? The word, the
loose, spoken word, has this consoling particularity: it is
close to sincerity, not in what it confesses, but in what it
claims to be and in what it pursues.

So I had to avoid turning my diary into a confession. I
had to show myself 'in action', in my intention of imposing
myself on the reader in a certain way, in my desire to create
myself with everyone looking on. 'This is how I would like
to be for you,' and not 'This is how I am.'

This may be the hidden aim of every writer who keeps a
diary. But it is only the 'hidden' aim. In my opinion, modern literature is the art of speaking plainly.

So far we have dealt with the personal aspect of my diary.
But it covers a far wider field. In it there are some main clues.

A certain classification has been proposed:

a. What I write about myself to throw myself into relief, to explain myself, or to provoke the reader's indignation, to surprise him, astonish him . . . the impressions, memories, accounts of journeys, confessions and secrets (because there are some of those, too).

b. Commentaries on my work and my polemic with the critics.

c. My war with literature and art, in general; the attacks on pure poetry, on painting, on Paris . . .

d. My war against philosophy and, particularly, against Existentialism, Catholicism, Marxism, and, more recently, against Structuralism.

e. My war against Poland and secondary cultures.

f. My observations on man, creature and creator of Form, an inadequate, immature being.

g. The eccentricities, the little lies, the jokes, the hoaxes—games with the reader.

h. The pages of an exclusively artistic nature—humour and lyricism, principally.

I have nothing against this classification, provided all the little a's and b's are well mixed up. Because my diary is a hodgepodge and nearly every single sentence can serve several gods at the same time.

When I look back at my diary I try to understand why my 'self' proved so aggressive as soon as it was set free. Indeed, however virulent I may have been in my former works, only there did I indulge in open criticism of modern culture. My audacity amazes me. And the nonchalance of this offensive, as well as its bitterness!

Was it not because this 'self' living on the other side of the ocean was so insignificant, so marginal, so anonymous? I had nothing to lose. I could write whatever passed through my head—nobody cared. And even if I was an artist (though an unrecognized one) and a poet, I was not a man of letters if, by this term, one means someone who has been introduced into the world of letters, someone with a certain know-how peculiar to this world, someone who has been trained at a particular school which alone entitles him to belong (meta-phorically) to the World Society of Men of Letters. At the basis of this aggression was the fact that my natural prefer-ence for a strictly private life, led all on my own, was sup-ported by my social position and my exile in the Argentine.

I was nothing, so I could do anything.

In the realms of culture, the following happens: as long as we keep to the rules of the game, everything is respectable and worthy of consideration. But as soon as we break the rules, the game is spoiled.

In the morning, a cultured man leafs through an intel-lectual review at breakfast and reads an important discussion between a structuralist and an existentialist. It is so intel-ligent that it is impossible to conclude that it is simply stu-pid—stupid because our two thinkers pretend to be more knowledgeable than they are. In fact they know very little and what they know they only know partially (indeed, how can one know anything in any other way?).

So, after reading with a tedious interest this stupid knowl-edgeable discussion, our *homo sapien* goes to town to see an exhibition of Picasso or (if you'd rather) Titian. And there he participates fervently, *but* distractedly: he is enchanted, *but* as if the whole thing had nothing to do with him. He falls to his knees, *but* it is as if he didn't fall. Then he tears himself away from Beauty with regret, *but* with relief. Once he is back at home, he seizes the latest novel, *but* it's as though he weren't reading it. He yawns. Looks out of the window. Closes the novel, takes *Ulysses* out of his library and reads without reading. He gets up, goes out for lunch, and, in cultured company, engages in intelligent conversation, not snobbishly, frankly, modestly, *but.* . . .

That's enough. You see, don't you? It's all a matter of this *but* which seeps through the rules of the game. My diary does not propose to delve into our culture, to enrich it, but to see whether it fits us, whether it remains down here, on earth, with us or whether it has broken away, soared into the sky, and is making us dizzy. It isn't culture that interests me so much as our relationship with it. My starting point is misleadingly simple: each of us plays at being cleverer and more mature than he is.

This may look like a mere denunciation of snobbery. Snobbery? Yes, that too. But something infinitely more important is at stake. An almost greater alienation than that brought about by machines. The accumulative and ascendant mechanisms of culture are very complicated and they operate outside ourselves, in the inter-human sphere.

I come from the country: that has something to do with my tastes. Think of my diary as the intrusion into European culture of a villager, of a Polish country gentleman, with all the mistrust, the common sense and the realism of a peasant. I inherited this mentality and it is very persistent. Despite so many years of exile and urban life, I still remain a Polish yokel. Somewhere in my diary, I have already noted that when I was young I pretended to be a land-owner in order to annoy the intellectuals, and, in order to annoy my family and the neighbours, I pretended to be an artist, a gypsy, an intellectual. I also wrote that I walked through culture like a farmer through his orchard, biting into a pear here, a prune there, and saying: this is good, that one isn't. I don't deny that this proprietor-consumer strolling through his orchard may irritate people, above all those who create, produce, sacrifice their body and soul on the altar of superior values. But if my diary can serve any purpose its first one is to oppose a rustic *laisser-faire* to the tensions which have accumulated in the metropolises of Europe and America.

I could define myself as a little Polish nobleman who has discovered his *raison d'etre* in what I would call distance from Form (and therefore distance from culture). The Polish nobleman, something of an anachronism, does not generally enjoy people's sympathy. So much the better! That's what I need. I would like to show that a critique of values made by a little nobleman can be effective.

What constitutes my strength? Well, the fact that everything in my life is so . . . so . . . haphazard . . . unfinished . . . fluid . . . inadequate . . . the fact that that is the real language of life and not the polished, elaborated, forced, and turgid language which others use.

I am a little like an aspirin relieving congestion. Or do you doubt that I, the author of *Ferdydurke*, *The Marriage*, *Pornografia*, am a nobleman? A revolutionary, an iconoclast, a blasphemer, an *avant-garde* writer, you may say, but no nobleman!

But don't you think that the *avant-garde* practised by a nobleman, a moderate conservative, inspires greater confidence? It is not desirable for a hairdresser to be like all the other hairdressers: a hairdresser is far more convincing when he thinks and acts like a colonel—and a colonel when he resembles a pharmacist. Art is always better off when it doesn't come from an artistic milieu. I repeat: to reassemble contradictions is the best method of creation.

I don't see why a country gentleman should not be the most modern man in the world . . . if he treats himself in a truly modern manner.

I emphasize my rustic background because that seems to me the most creative element in my diary; and that is where criticism starts. Although this criticism . . . is not so simple. Indeed, my campaign against intensity couldn't itself be intense, my diary couldn't become what it wanted to put into question, it couldn't turn into all that it was fighting against. This critique had to be casual and relaxed . . . and it had to be relaxed even in its relaxation.

So the very strength of the campaign lay in its weakness. Paradoxical, isn't it? But I had always been aware of the inanity of all argumentation, and I knew that one couldn't get very far with reasoning, that it was better to seduce, to provoke with a certain tone, a certain spirit, a certain attitude. So the confusion of my diary, the combination of serious themes with unimportant details, the avoidance of all forms of 'greatness', this stroll through an orchard, are all nothing but a bait, they are there to seduce, to produce a certain style, a certain tonality.

I knew that that was the most important thing. Many

young people came to sit at my table, first in the cafés of Poland, then in the cafés of the Argentine. Some had a pugnacious temperament. They clashed violently with me. Well, it took me some time to understand why some of my opponents took so long and were so reluctant to introduce me to their family or their friends. And then, one fine day, I discovered why: the opponents had copied my way of talking and joking and were having a great success behind my back. When I happened to meet the cousin of one of them, she exclaimed: 'But you talk just like Alberto!'

Then Alberto's arguments no longer scared me. I knew I had conquered him. Oh! I'm far from thinking that Sartre or Foucault would ever create such difficulties for me with their cousins, but I'll gradually seep through. I don't want to be like a wave breaking against a cliff, but, in my diary, I want to be like water that soaks, drenches, saturates. . . .

9

PORNOGRAFIA

Time passed. 1955. I still—Lord have mercy on me!—
worked as a secretary at the Banco Polaco. I did so with ever
greater difficulty. I could stand it no longer. In a spurt of
desperate heroism, I left the bank! It was a leap in the dark.
My savings amounted to about two thousand dollars, I had
no job for the future, nothing to hold on to!

Well, my first two years away from the bank were heav-
enly! A holiday every day! Sunday from morning to night.
And the hand presiding over my fate was benevolent.
Immediately after giving notice, I managed to obtain a few
little subsidies from various sources thanks to which I could
count on a very small, but very vital, minimum. So I could
get down to writing. And since Peron's dictatorship fell at
that very moment, the winds of freedom blew around me
from every side!

Write? Go on writing? Writing what? As always I started
scribbling something, overwhelmed by the uncertainty, the
ignorance, the depressing misery which hit me every time I
started a book. It gradually grew richer, more intense, and
thus emerged a new form, a new work, the novel which

I entitled *Pornografia*. It wasn't too bad a title at the time, but today, with the invasion of pornography, it has become rather banal and certain translators have chosen to call it *Seduction*.

At that time I bought a typewriter, a semi-portable Remington, brand-new, a very distinguished colour, and it was as though I had bought a Rolls Royce. I was in an agonizing quandary for three whole days: should I buy it or should I make do with the second-hand Olivetti I was offered?

I typed *Pornografia* on this Remington. I wrote it out by hand first and then copied it out on the typewriter, making little changes.

My works 'come about', they 'happen' to be written, they almost write themselves. And *Pornografia* became a necessity.

The fundamental choice of an artist lies in the apprehension of a certain beauty—a hidden secret lying dormant. There is no doubt that I came to literature seduced and fascinated by this certain type of beauty which influenced all my mental speculations, even the most abstract. So the time would have to come when I could make my way along the paths of art to that sacred place where my charms and spells were celebrated.

You know from my diary how difficult it was for me to break with youth. This break came very late. I continued to look and feel young until I was forty. I belong to that race of people who have never known middle age. I tasted age the moment I said farewell to youth.

I don't believe that I am alone in experiencing such adventures with beauty and youth. I give the impression of being an egotist enclosed in his ivory tower, but I hope I have succeeded in showing to what extent I am a child of my time. All these plunges into the spheres of our intimate mythology, and this overthrow of tastes and tendencies which characterizes the present age and thanks to which youth has recently gained the upper hand and the son has stolen a march on the father, were sensed by me at their birth, during the First World War, when they were barely perceptible. Yes, at that period I already felt myself to be in the grips of this metamorphosis. I remember rather ashamedly the time when people used to say to me, 'Be a man!' This never aroused my enthusiasm. I, a boy, loved youth as though I were already old. At a later age, youth's pressure on me increased enormously, but at the same time I discovered that I was not the only victim. Something was happening all around me, in people, something to do with youth. Perhaps such changes, which take place in our own narcissistic nature, are important to the development of humanity.

As for the subsequent adventures I had with the two goddesses, Youth and Beauty, I could sum them up in four theses, which I consider most revealing:

The first: *youth is inferiority*

The second: *youth is beauty*

The third (and how thrilling!): *so, beauty is inferiority*

The fourth (dialectical): *man is suspended between God and youth*.

I arrived at these theses little by little. As always. But whereas as my other ideas grew within me quietly, my ideas on youth struck me like momentary, almost dramatic flashes, causing an intense excitement in the darkest corners of my being. Yet, if I say that I came to them little by little it is because they assaulted me, only to disappear and then reappear again.

I yielded very soon and very suddenly to the truth that 'youth is inferiority', as to an indubitable fact. Yes, to be young meant to be weaker, inferior, inadequate, immature . . . to be beneath the level of everything of value . . . and (careful!) even beneath oneself (in the future!). So youth must bow down to maturity, and the rule of the Adult over the Young is just. And, of course, it was youth and nothing else which pushed me towards all the other inferiorities, degradations, social and even spiritual.

Subsequently it was revealed to me that 'youth is beauty'. I say 'revealed' because there is a great difference between the normal awareness of any old cliché and the act of penetrating its live, creative content. I experienced one of these revelations in the Tatras. It was in the summer (I was well over twenty at the time), and I went up to the peak of Kasprowy-Wierch in the Zakopane funicular. I slept in an empty shelter where there was nothing but walls, two rows of beds, a heap of mattresses on the floor, and clouds of mist trailing on the ground, muting everything, gluing-up one's eyes. It was cold and damp, benumbingly cold. On the third day, the weather improved and, bathing in air and light, I descended, if I am not mistaken, to Hala Gasienicowa (I get lost in those mountains nowadays) where, in another shelter, I came across two groups of school children on an excursion, one of boys, the other of girls. There was nothing extraordinary about them, but they radiated something that suggested the possibility of seduction. Their air of incomplete-ness, their infantile fragility, suddenly increased their power to charm, rather than attenuated it, and the two groups changed into two choirs. A melodic, inspired hymn burst from their lips and became Beauty. There was something 'interior' in this voiceless hymn, and this gave me the idea that beauty, the beauty of the youth of the human species, is something special, something 'interior', as opposed to the beauty of the outer world. I recently read the reminiscences of an eminent painter for whom an ugly old woman was a more interesting subject for a picture than a beautiful girl. I don't deny this: the patterns of lines and warts is undoubtedly richer than a smooth face . . . but shouldn't we preserve strictly human beauty, that which our species cultivates in its breast, and repeats continuously in the seductive form of a boy or a girl, from any confusion with 'objective beauty'? We have this original beauty within ourselves, it is ours and it demands *something else* from us, a different approach. In the combination of these two types of beauty I believe that we can find one of the reasons why the school of modern painting has such a pernicious aesthetic and spiritual aspect.

Why should youth, inferior and imperfect, be more beautiful? Well, this is perfectly comprehensible from the biological point of view, which makes the feeble, inferior, helpless being, who needs protection, appeal to the stronger. The mature man does not need to seduce; he is powerful, he dominates, he governs. Charm and beauty are the arms of the woman, the adolescent, the child.

But then we must deduce that . . . *beauty is synonymous with inferiority*.

See how something artistically important can spring from

the confrontation of these two ideas? I cannot clearly recall the chronology of these initiations. I think it was at the end of my stay in the Argentine, by chance, during a conversation, that this formula occurred to me, although it had existed within me for some time. And I felt that it pierced me to the heart. The artist works in beauty as other people work in insurance companies or in farming, yet he doesn't necessarily know what beauty is . . . then suddenly, that little phrase, which occurred quite accidently, illuminated many, many things. I found it an adequate explanation for many of my phobias: that was why I detested religious painting (beauty was connected with virtue), why I hated the over-elaborate beauty of *haute couture*, of pure poetry and abstract art. Hence, also, my allergy towards moustaches and beards! That was why Beauty was a jewel for me, found in a gutter. And . . . and . . . how much more exciting it all appeared to me, devoid as it was of harmony and tedious perfection, lyrical and almost wild, what incalculable dynamism resided in that dethroned goddess chained to youth.

This may have corresponded to the hitherto little known tendencies of my time. It may well have been the hidden dream of the generation on the threshold of life. But the efforts of contemporary art to offer us an objective and abstract beauty appeared to me in this light as the tactics of an ostrich, or, I should rather say, of a hare. I talk as an artist. It has been said that 'it is impossible to combat what the soul has chosen'.

I mentioned all this in two chapters of my diary—in 1956, when I wrote about the Retiro, the harbour district of Buenos Aires. I then tended to see youth as a value in itself. But youth is beneath all value, the only value of youth is youth. And that is why, as I wrote a brief preface to the French edition of *Pornografia*, a phrase a little like this came to my mind: 'Man is suspended between God and youth'.

This means that man has two ideals, divinity and youth. He wants to be perfect, immortal, omnipotent. He wants to be God. And he wants to be in full bloom, fresh and pink, always to remain in the ascendant phase of his life—he wants to be young.

He aspires to perfection, but he is afraid of it because he knows that it is death. He rejects imperfection, but it attracts him because it is life and beauty.

There's nothing extraordinary about that—it's an idea like any other . . . but what a beacon for me!

For, as I write, I have a tendency—a subterranean, illegal tendency—to complete the natural development of immaturity towards maturity with a radically opposite trend, leading downwards, from maturity to immaturity. In *Ferdydurke*, one can see the extent to which, despite my efforts to become mature, I remained attached to immaturity. That has always tormented me. Man pursues two goals, he is torn between two poles. . . . Yes, of course the adult is the professor, the master of the youth. But does this adult not secretly frequent another school, where the youth dominates him? Would the furious dynamism of life, this compression (the source of its energy), be possible without it?

Our wars are wars of adolescents, I once wrote in my diary. The social order is based on violence, which is called military service, on the submission of the young to a blind discipline, to the will of the officer. Would it be possible for certain men to dominate others without the suppleness, the lightness of youth? And, finally, blind obedience is double-edged, it is reciprocal: he who commands becomes the slave of the slave. And it is by this reciprocal submission that a whole potential of energy, recklessness and impetuosity is created; the superhuman and the inhuman arise from it tinged with lightness, innocence. The participation of youth in our adult life, the participation of immaturity, has not yet been sufficiently brought to light.

It may seem that I have so far been somewhat reticent about 'immaturity' which, together with Form, constitutes my principal idea. Am I not, you may ask, emphasizing 'Form' in this case too? I think it is easier to approach my universe from the side of Form. Besides, I am sick of the gross misunderstandings to which immaturity has given rise. Poor thing, it becomes all too frequently an excuse for intellectual laziness. 'Oh, Gombrowicz makes no sense, he's so childish and immature', say my critics. This may have something to do with the influence of structuralism, to which I am opposed insofar as it is a product of science (I, an artist, am by nature anti-scientific, anti-objective). Yet I also regard it as an ally who shares my fascination with Form. I greeted structuralism with enthusiasm, just as I had previously welcomed existentialism, for they have both chosen streams in which I swim myself.

Let us move on to *Pornografia*.

The hero of the novel, Frederick, is a Christopher Columbus who departs in search of unknown continents. What is he searching for? This new beauty, this new poetry, hidden between the adult and the young man. He is the poet of an awareness carried to the extreme, or, at least, that's how I wanted him to be. But it is difficult to understand one another nowadays! Certain critics saw him as Satan, no more, no less, while others, mainly Anglo-Saxons, were content with a more trivial definition—a voyeur. My Frederick is neither Satan nor a voyeur: he is more like a theatrical producer, or even a chemist, trying to obtain a new and magical alcohol by various combinations between individuals.

What happens in *Pornografia*? We, Frederick and I, two middle-aged gentlemen, see a young couple, a girl and a boy, who seem to be made for each other, welded to each other with a striking and reciprocal sex appeal. But as far as they're concerned they might not even have noticed it: it is drowned, we might say, in their youthful incapacity for fulfilment (the inexperience peculiar to their age). We, the older ones, are excited by it, we would like the charm to take shape. And, with due precautions, and keeping up appearances, we start to help them. But our efforts lead us nowhere; they founder in that sphere of pre-reality where they reside and which characterizes them—in that antechamber of their existence.

And then? Let us glide over the cunning devices of the matchmaker-producer, who is also a voyeur, but a poet-voyeur. The smoke that rises from this magic enclosure intoxicates us more and more and, exasperated by the indifference of the two children, it occurs to us that, failing physical possession, sin, a common sin, can tie them together and—oh joy!—can tie *us* to *them*, like accomplices, despite the difference of age.

Towards the end of this novel, set in martyred, German-occupied Poland, we, the adults, find ourselves obliged to kill an important member of the Resistance who has lost his nerve and might squeal. Yet this is more than we can do. We, the adults, weighed down by our awareness and our seriousness, know what death is. But someone light will accomplish it lightly—and we entrust this murder to the boy. In his hands, it will become juvenile.

Frederick organizes this youthful crime by drawing the girl into it. Thus it will become the common sin, mature and young, which will bind us all together. At the last moment, not knowing what to do with another boy who is hanging around with no definite role, our matchmaker-producer simply kills him. In order to improve the taste, in order to improve the broth with this extra piece of fresh meat, so that blood-stained youth can reinforce that other youth, his equal in age. . . .

A desperate struggle between the mature wish to *accomplish* something and that light, careless, irresponsible quality of youth. The wish is all the more stimulated by the fact that what it strikes puts up no resistance. And weakness proves stronger than strength. Finally the lightness of a seventeen-year-old removes the weight from the crimes and the sins: the novel ends in unfulfillment. It has been said that the end lacks intensity, but that's what I wanted. Everything has to dissolve.

I may be wrong to propose systems like that. An author should never comment too much on his own work. But how else can one save oneself from totally erroneous interpretations, made as every critic pleases? The reader should know, by and large, how I managed to write a novel and what it's made of.

If someone put me up against the wall and asked me what

beauty Frederick is pursuing in *Pornografia,* I would say: one doesn't really know. People may see my enhancement of youth as proof of my homosexual proclivities: I can hardly deny this. Yet I must make an observation: is it possible for the most masculine man, who loves women, to remain entirely insensitive to the beauty of a boy? And again: is homosexuality—that age-old, eternal, recurrent phenomenon—a mere deviation? And if this deviation is so common, so universal, does it not have something really magical about it? Does it not happen that man, enchanted by youth, and for ever fascinated and enthralled by the idea of the boy, prefers to take refuge in the arms of a woman because, in a certain sense, she is the boy he is allowed? This may seem exaggerated, but it contains a grain of truth.

In many countries we are now witnessing a revolt of youth. In a strange way this seems to confirm what I have been writing for many years about the relationship between the young and the adult which will, I believe, become increasingly productive and dramatic. In a sense these recent events do reflect some of my ideas.[*]

---

[*] Here is an interesting view contained in an article on the student revolts by K. A. Jelenski, the greatest Polish expert on Gombrowicz:

Admittedly no one foresaw the student 'revolution'. No politician or sociologist, or any of the numerous specialists of the student world. Yet there is one work of literature which adumbrated this revolt: the work of Gombrowicz.

In *Ferdydurke* we have the praise of immaturity, the rejection of Form, the critique of 'imposed' culture, Mientus' 'fraternisation' with the stable-lad.

In *Trans-Atlantyk* we have the opposition between father and son.

In *Pornografia* we have the solidarity of the young in violence.

And finally *Operetta.* Here the ruins of the Himalay princes' castle and the degeneration of Hufnagel's ideological revolution really seem to be a poetic illustration of the recent events. But in the finale Albertine's 'resurrection' expresses faith in the potential force of youth:

Youthful nudity forever, hail!

Hail, youth forever nude!

As I said just now, for me youth is inferior and inadequate in everything except for one thing: in that it is young, it is youth 'in itself'. So there is nothing surprising about the fact that the action of the young, in as far as it constitutes a political, social, or ideological programme, should be of such poor quality. But what happens is that these riots are really a blind outburst, outside ideology—a sort of eruption. That's youth, yes. In order to understand my attitude one must look at things from an artistic rather than from a moral point of view. A boy who throws stones is all right, he isn't artistically shocking. But a boy who makes speeches and tries to change the world is simply naïve and pretentious. That's bad.

Oh dear! This crisis may have a certain authenticity about it, but it has also given rise to the most grotesque and intolerable lies! And why? Because this revolt of the young is really the work of adults. Look: a few hundred youths start a riot for some reason or other at Nanterre or anywhere else, and they give vent to their rancour against society. There's nothing important about that. It's rather silly. But then the papers, the radio, get hold of an exciting, spicy theme worth reporting, and the pamphleteers, the sociologists, the philosophers, the politicians blacken reams of paper. 'What is the spirit of the young?' 'I don't know what to tell my son.' 'The young condemn us!' 'What is their secret?' 'Modern man is at a loss.' It sounds good, it sounds profound. They said that to start with there were five hundred negroes and five thousand journalists behind Stokely Carmichael in the United States. Well, the same applies to Cohn-Bendit. And, at that age, it's difficult not to think oneself an instrument of history when one sees oneself on the front page of every newspaper. The young believed it. They got swollen-headed. And the adults got into a funk. The monster of youth, as it appears to us now, is of our own (adult) invention.

This crisis is far more an adult crisis than a crisis of the young. Above all it shows a remarkable weakening in the mature man when confronted with the young man.

We, the adults, feel that our superiority is at an end. The principle of authority, which has always kept the son in a state of passive obedience, is beginning to founder. Youth appears to us more and more as an active and creative force, in its own way, by its own means. But the nature of this force and the part it has to play escapes us. The problem of the generation gap, of the ascending and descending phases of life, of the Mature and the Immature, of the Superior and the Inferior, no—it's not that simple. It's difficult and obscure. The adult feels himself threatened by the young— undermined by a different reality which is piercing him—a reality which may operate like a permanent dematuring process, like a reduction, or even like an oppressive, condensing, contracting element . . . let's leave it at that. In any event, the mature man faced with youth, has lost his superiority which, apart from every rational concept, is simply due to the fact that he is more *developed*.

It is funny to see all these professors, thinkers, and others, dazed, terrified, determined to 'understand' the young, to be 'with it'. What cowardice! How pathetic! Instead of taking these revolts for what they are, an outburst, an eruption of high spirits, they endow them with conscious, elevated aims. 'We are old, retarded failures and they want a better society—they are the future, the *nouvelle vague*!' All this ends in a caricature: on the one hand there is a terrifying Youth, powerful, reckless, prophetic, enlightened, vindictive, angel or demon, and on the other there is a puny little man whose trousers are falling off—the adult. And the one feels ridiculous before the other.

As far as I'm concerned this is the most important aspect. It means that a bad Form is imposing itself between the generations. Why bad? Because it doesn't correspond to reality. And what is reality? Don't ask me too much, I'm incapable of replying. But I can say in all sincerity that the authentic presence of the young being cannot manifest itself on the collective, social, political or ethical level. Today we are tempted to see only the social reality of man. But no. That's too narrow and superficial. There are many things that take place in secret, in a private arena, and it is here that a youth appears as the herald of a type of beauty, of poetry, as somebody drawing us downwards.

No doubt, however, political forces will do all they can to gain control of this force which is extremely effective in the streets. This miserable flirtatiousness is going to falsify the adult-youth relationship still more. This is why I am pessimistic. We must expect a long period of stupidity, of heartbreaking rhetoric, discomfort and maladroitness. This always happens whenever a bad, irritating, artificial relationship extends between two people or two generations.

That is what I can say from a strictly 'formal' point of view. But I would like to add: the student revolts in Eastern Europe have nothing to do with those in the West. The former are the result of misery, the latter of satiety.

10

COSMOS

In 1957, Asian 'flu put an end to the euphoria I had experienced since leaving the bank. From then on, asthma started to suffocate me, though at first it gave me some respite. And I began to feel my age, too. My books slowly made their way in Europe. How much longer would I stay in the Argentine?

Six years. Six more years before my feathers grew and I took wing. April 1963. The Ford Foundation invited me to spend a year in Berlin together with several other writers from various countries. Fifteen hundred dollars a month and no obligations. My financial problems were solved. I left. Farewell, Argentine!

When I boarded the *Federico* off Buenos Aires I had behind me twenty-three years and two hundred and twenty-six days of the Argentine (I counted them) and with me, in my suitcase, the text of an unfinished novel: *Cosmos*. The fourth after *Ferdydurke*, *Trans-Atlantyk,* and *Pornografia*. This novel won me the International Publishers' Prize, the most important literary award after the Nobel Prize, but I had no premonition of this as I danced with it on the Atlantic waves. Prizes weren't my strong point. I was almost sixty and

I still hadn't won a single one. I had gotten used to the idea that they weren't for me.

Cosmos? I'm getting a little tired of reviewing my books one by one. For me, *Cosmos* is black, primarily black, something like a black stream, turbulent, full of whirlpools, obstacles, and flooded areas, carrying a mass of refuse, and, in this stream, a besotted man, at the mercy of the waters, trying to decipher and to understand so that he can assemble what he sees into some whole. Blackness, terror, and night. Night crossed by a violent passion, an unnatural love. What do I know? It seems to me that this dramatic aspect of *Cosmos* will only be fully perceptible in many years' time. It is an austere book, and I have less fun in it than in my other works.

Once a Tolstoy or a Balzac could write for almost everyone; that has become virtually impossible for a contemporary writer, for the simple reason that we no longer share a common universe. There are a dozen different universes competing for our readers. How can we find a language comprehensible to a conservative Catholic, an existentialist atheist, a 'realist', a man whose conscious patterns of thought have been formulated by Husserl or Freud and one whose artistic sensibility has been developed in the shadow of surrealism? Different realities, different ways of seeing and feeling. In the four corners of these different horizons the whole diversity of our temperaments appears. The time of ordinary reading is over.

Cosmos is capable of upsetting me, even of frightening me. Why? Because, during my lifetime, I have created for myself a special sensibility towards Form and, quite frankly, the fact of having five fingers on one hand scares me. Why five? Why not 327, 584, 598, 208, 854? And why not all these quantities at the same time? And why fingers? For me nothing is more fantastic than to *be* here, now, and to be *as I am*, defined, concrete, and not someone else. And I fear Form as if it were a wild animal! Do other people share my anxiety? To what extent? If a man doesn't see Form as I see it, in its autonomy, its perpetual malleability, its creative fury, its caprices and its perversions, its accumulations and its dissolutions, its intricacies and continual confusions, what can *Cosmos* mean to him? If, in the future, such a notion of Form becomes more widespread, *Cosmos* may make him shudder.

It seems to me that the future of my works depends essentially on a certain evolution in the way of looking at the world, an evolution which may or may not come about.

I already owe a great deal to the last war. After it, people began to read me differently. Yet I am not quite sure that that evolution will continue for long enough to allow them to assimilate *Cosmos* fully. I am almost sure, however. Every sign in heaven and earth points to it—the crisis of ideologies, the ever more advanced interest in Form, the most recent artistic trends. Only that isn't enough for me.

If this increasing 'formalism' is not counter-balanced by humanism, that is to say by the human element, by human anguish, poetry, passion, my work and I will perish in this new Sahara. I won't die alone, however. I fear this because of the growing mechanization of culture brought about by the academic mass production of professors, doctors, bachelors of arts . . . but I don't think all this can last very long.

Despite my attack on painters, my treatment of Form is, in a sense, not dissimilar to that of modern painting. The contemporary painter has learnt to decompose the visible world into its elements of colour and line from which he elaborates a new and arbitrary composition. I do more or less the same thing, although my world is never totally decomposed. And besides, the painter's brush leaves it at that, the painter cannot return to man a world that has been broken thus. He gives man the 'pure' pattern of Form to contemplate, and it all ends there. The word, on the other hand, is an incomparably richer, more powerful tool than the paintbrush. It disposes of several different means of action and, use of the word in its fullest sense makes the re-humanization of Form possible. It has been said that painting is a hundred years ahead of literature. It will be disastrous for literature if it ever takes the same road, for it is also to the fact that painting is such a bad master for the writer that we must attribute the improverishment of recent French writing.

In literature, which, fortunately, is not pure art, but is more than art, it is permissible to do what painting does in addition to something more important, something which is the very opposite of painting. One can be all the more human the more one is inhuman, all the more concrete the more one is abstract. Yes, contradiction, the spirit of contradiction, is very necessary. Life must once again be opposed to art and to Form.

In *Cosmos* not only can I decompose the world into elements of form: I can also recreate man's reaction—the normal reaction of a normal man of flesh and blood faced by this process of decomposition, his fear, his despair, or his enchantment, in such a way that it is again man, and not Form, that is at the heart of my work. With me, Form can be heaven or hell. But with a painter Form must simply be 'as it is'. If the canvas could present us with Form 'as it is' together with the bordeom of the man who cotmplates it, I might not have been so much in opposition.

In my opinion it is on this rehumanization of inhumanity that the literature of tomorrow depends. Will it swing in a void, drawing bizarre figures, or will it find a firm ground under its feet? If I'm right, I win the game: otherwise . . . I might win too, but in that case I shall be read differently.

We have liberated the demon of Form and the time has come to take him by the horns.

In a sense the contradictory opinions about *Cosmos* stem from my ambivalent attitude towards Form, which I liberate from man and, at the same time, subject to man. For some, the development of the story is unnatural, forced, artificial, while others complain that it is told in too realistic a way, reminiscent of traditional literature.

Forced? Artificial? Those who say that have not noticed that *Cosmos* is not an ordinary novel which tells a story—let us say a tragic love story. The main theme of the novel is the very formation of this story, in other words, the formation of a reality . . . in it we see how a certain reality endeavours to arise from our associations, indolently, awkwardly . . . in a jungle of misunderstandings and erroneous interpretations. And at each moment, the awkward construction is lost in chaos. *Cosmos* is a novel which creates itself, as it is written.

Realism? Tradition? These are the accusations of those who have not noticed that, in *Cosmos*, I am telling the simple story of a simple student.

This student goes to spend his holidays as a paying guest in a house where he meets two women, one has a hideous mouth which has been ruined by a motor car accident, while the other has an attractive mouth. The two mouths are associated in his mind and become an obsession. On the other hand, he has seen a sparrow hanging from a wire and a piece of wood hanging from a thread. . . . And all this, a little out of bordeom, a little out of curiosity, a little out of love, out of violent passion, starts dragging him towards a certain means of action . . . to which he abandons himself, but not without scepticism. What is so extraordinary about all this? It can happen to anyone. Why should I have used anything more than a straightforward narrative form to tell this story?

Cosmos is an ordinary introduction to an extraordinary world, to the wings of the world, if you like.

Here too, I suppose, I appear as an *avant-garde* conservative. The spirit of contradiction again, no doubt: I always manage to be 'between'. My writing is based on traditional models. In a sense *Ferdydurke* is a parody of a *conte philosophique* in the manner of Voltaire. *Trans-Atlantyk* is the parody of an old-fashioned tale in an antiquated and stereotyped style. *Pornografia* is a continuation of the débonnaire 'Polish country novel'. *Cosmos* is something of a thriller. My plays are a parody of Shakespeare and my last play is based on traditional operettas.

If I rely on traditional forms it is because they are the most perfect and the reader is already used to them. But please don't forget—it is important—that with me Form is always a parody of Form. I use it, but I escape from it.

Yes, I look for the connection between these old literary forms which are readable and the newest, the very latest perception of the world. To smuggle the most modern goods in an old-fashioned wagon like *Trans-Atlantyk* or *Pornografia* is what I like doing!

I don't think that form and content are one and the same thing by any means. In the most limited sense they may be, perhaps, but not in the deepest sense, where man battles against Form.

The *nouveau roman*? The latest experiments in novel form? What do I think of them? I'm no critic and I wouldn't be one for anything on earth. My 'critical' attitude towards new novels is expressed in the decisive and definitive fact that I am unable to read them. Why? Because they bore me. They bore me and that's that. I might at the most ask myself what the cause of this boredom is, if there is a deeper motivation for it. But you'll agree that such an analysis would never be serious. It is very unfair to pass judgement on something one hasn't read.

Who knows? This may be why these books are so resistant to criticism. They are so boring that they are unreadable, so one can't criticize them.

I'm not being spiteful, no. God forbid! Assertions as simple as mine can only be useful to the extent in which they are sincere and serious. If they were merely spiteful what use would they be? And I really feel uncomfortable about having to deal so unceremoniously with disinterested authors of such incontestable quality. But a fact is a fact, there's nothing to be done about it. I have the greatest respect for facts.

But though I have not read these books I shall tell you what I don't like about them. What justifies my boredom will not, of course, necessarily justify yours.

Primo: it is all theory. Intellectual. Fabricated. Of scientific inspiration. Abstract. Art on its knees before science, which leads it wherever it likes.

Secundo: it all lives in a vacuum. One man writes for the other. It's a mutual admiration society.

Tertio: it's arid. Their aim will always be economy, purity, quintessence, 'art for art's sake', 'writing for writing's sake', 'the word for the word's sake'.

Quarto: it's naïve. Faith in art. Faith in the myth 'I am a creator', 'I am an artist'.

Quinto: it's monotonous. They are all doing more or less the same thing.

Sexto: it's all in the air. It doesn't have its feet on the ground. Abstraction. Obstinacy. Solipsism. Onanism. Disloyalty towards reality.

This occured to me . . . like that, in general. . . .

Imagine an intelligent student full of respect for science, his head stuffed with concepts, theories, abstract ideas, enclosed in his own little circle, a concentrated, studious, honest, high-minded, yes, high-minded individual . . . and one who has an artistic vocation. He is going to start building a new model of art as a mechanic might make a motor car. Locked in his laboratory, what has he to fear? Life. Letting himself go. Pleasure. Enjoyment. Freedom. His work bores him to tears, but that doesn't matter, let's write, theory knows what's good for us more than practice! His work will bore others to tears, but that doesn't matter, let's write. According to the theory, it is we who have to adapt ourselves to the work, not the work to us! Hasn't it always been like that? What was unreadable yesterday, will be readable tomorrow. That's how it's always been and that's how it'll always be! Let's write!

From such an asceticism, incapable of enjoying life and unable to have fun, never seeking one's own or anybody else's pleasure, and still less a personal profit, from such high-mindedness, always ready for self-sacrifice, come the books of martyrs. This is martyrdom.

You have what you deserve: you have persecuted this wretched 'self' so often that you have reached an impersonal literature and hence an abstract, unreal, artificial, cerebral, cowardly, feeble literature, deprived of strength, vigour, freshness, originality, determined only to bore. Where are the good old days, when Rabelais wrote as a child might pee against a tree, to relieve himself? The old days when literature took a deep breath and created itself freely, among people, for people! These books may have sold more copies than mine, but what does that prove? A pseudo-creator gets his pseudo-reader! They are bought, they aren't read.

In a sense, of course, there are more similarities than differences between me and them. I, too, am difficult. I, too, write for the future. I, too, have theories, concepts. I, too, experiment. But I am a humourist, a joker, an acrobat, a provocateur. My works turn double somersaults to please. I am a circus, lyricism, poetry, horror, riots, games—what more do you want? I am difficult, I admit. When I can't be otherwise. But if there is a man who writes in the mortal terror of being boring, I am he! Those sessions during which writers read their works aloud amaze me. I would be incapable of reading a single page of mine, so scared would I be of making people yawn! Today, in the bureaucratic atmosphere in which we live, the French aphorism *Tous les genres sont bons, sauf les genres ennuyeux* is no longer a bugbear. This is a pity.

After all, I may be wrong to stick my nose into all this. What point is there in declaring war on these young novelists? They and I are members of the same family, it's amongst them that I find my best friends and readers. And that might harm me, above all in Paris, for they have the Parisian critics at their feet . . . and how agreeable it would be to say: enough! Things have come to a pretty pass! There's room for everybody, variety is desirable. 'Let each man do according to the dictates of his soul and all will turn out for the best' . . . . such evangelical maxims are quite good for the digestion.

But! . . . At the Café Rex in Buenos Aires, where I went to play chess, I used to see a very thin, unhealthily shy young Brazilian who talked so quietly that nobody knew what he was saying. Out of politeness, people answered him at random and an inconsequential conversation might ensue. One day I went up to him and said: 'You know that you've never spoken to anyone in your life? Everyone lies to you.' This surprised him . . . and he muttered something which I didn't hear.

You know, the artist is an individual who is systematically tricked from the first word he writes. I, too, am incapable of telling someone who gives me his work to read—a work written by the sweat of his brow, the fruit of endless patience—that I can't read it. You get along with the help of little lies: 'Yes, there are some interesting passages, and even, in a sense, very . . . though possibly . . . ' etc. You know that you are lying and you know that others will lie and that this wretched individual is going to ruin his life by living on little lies. These will envelope him increasingly as time goes by. They might even enable him to enjoy a seemingly passable position in the artistic world which will breed new lies, and so on.

Not even the best of us can escape from this. A permanent lie gnaws at us. The critic, the friend, the stranger, the editor, the connoisseur, the admirer, every reader . . . they all lie, lie, lie. . . . *To contradict*, even on little matters, is the supreme necessity of art today.

11

FINALLY . . .

On 22 April 1963, I landed in Europe at Barcelona. The next day I was in Cannes and was soon rushing towards Paris in the Mistral Express. I got out at the Gare de Lyon and there, I, an anonymous, Argentinian, Gombrowicz, was naturally assimilated by the writer Gombrowicz who had patiently matured in Paris, almost behind my back, and who awaited me there.

But in my little hotel room near the Opéra, I had to open my window . . . I was suffocating.

Until then I had not fully realized what made my separation from the Argentine so agonizing. I now began to understand. For me, Europe was death. This return meant that I had reached the end of the road. I was finished.

Berlin. I was at last approaching the demoniacal origin of everybody's ruination, including mine. I survived in Berlin for just over a year, a doubtful smile on my lips, a stone's throw from Poland, sullen and ashen. 'Flu. A slight attack of 'flu with a low temperature, but the doctor told me: spend a few days in hospital, it will be easier for me to look after you there. So, on 22 February (the twos) 1964 (the sum of the digits is 20), I went into hospital. For a few days? For two months, I couldn't get rid of this 'flu, it wasn't one, it was four attacks of 'flu which assailed me, combined with other ailments. Finally, poisoned by antibiotics—I had lost forty pounds—more dead than alive, I flew back to France.

After spending several months at Royaumont near Paris I settled in Vence, in the Alpes-Maritimes, above the sea, between Nice and Cannes.

I gradually recovered my strength. My Argentinian penury was over. At least my monthly income was higher than a hundred and fifty dollars. A fine sunset, a superb autumn, an abundant harvest. More and more translations. The International Publishers' Prize. Comfort. A little flat, a little car, a wife, a family life. So here I was, a 'writer', and, now that I was over sixty, I could say what any student can say after obtaining his degree in medicine or engineering: 'I am someone, I've made it.'

Yes, but the hand (which had rescued me from the war and deposited me in the Argentine) only allowed me to gaze at these sweets through a window, a window made of lack . . . of lack of air. The hand imposed asceticism on me and I accepted it without flinching. I had always known, from the start, that literature could give me no material advantage: I had never counted on it.

Operetta. I was already in Vence when I finished *Cosmos.* The third volume of my diary (the years 1961 to 1966) was published in Polish (but not in Poland, where I am still banned). To my amazement my plays, which Jorge Lavelli had rescued from oblivion in Paris, appeared on other stages, where they had quite a success. I then got out my rough drafts of *Operetta*, a play I had begun when I was still working in the bank—and which I had abandoned—and with which I struggled again in Tandil, and which I had once again hidden in a drawer.

The reef against which all my efforts crashed was the style of the *Operetta*. Divinely idiotic and perfectly sclerotic, like all monumental and crystallized styles, it tolerated nothing that was not perfectly integrated. In an *Operetta*, the characters, the story, the universe, the myths must be *Operetta*-like, and I tried to put too many things into it. Only when I managed to insert all these contents—clothes, fashion, and so on—into the theatrical language peculiar to the *Operetta* did the play become more harmonious.

Operetta has not yet been performed,[*] the translations not finished. Those who have read it say different things about it: some say that it is cruel and tragic, others that it is overflowing with an optimistic faith in the perpetually renascent and naked youth of humanity.

Politics. You know, a friend wrote me an indignant letter saying that *Operetta* is anti-left, and therefore right-wing! I had never been told anything of the sort before. Never, until then, had my works been interpreted in a political perspective, in the West, at least. Of course, *Operetta* is neither left- nor right-wing; it is, I agree, the proclamation of the bankruptcy of all political ideology, of the

---

[*] Since this was written. *Operetta* has been translated into several languages and has received two major European productions: Theatre Nationale Populaire in Paris, in 1970, and the Teatro Stabile dell'Aquila in Italy, in 1969. (Ed.).

bankruptcy of *clothing*.

But am I really apolitical? How can an artist be political? Would you like a statue by Phidias to make a speech against imperialism, a symphony of Mozart to sign protests, the Mona Lisa to hold forth about the colour problem? Leave this group of visionaries, dreamers and poets in peace. Let them do what they like! We accept mountaineers without asking them to make a statement about the Russian revolution from the peak of Mont Blanc. So let a group of artists climb in their own style on the peaks where the view is extensive, nebulous and slightly *sub specie aeternitatis*.

Let us leave the artist alone with his work. Let us be discreet. Art is a difficult enterprise which is carried out in the twilight.

Yet I am not in favour of pure art. As a writer, I am hardly entitled to refer to the Mona Lisa or to Mozart because, I admit, literature is an impure form of art. Language can be used by art, but it can also express something else. But literature is also art, and that which is divine must indeed be rendered unto God. Only the rest must be rendered unto Caesar.

If an artist's pen strays onto the ground of political ideology I, for one, am not going to read him (in this domain I prefer a treatise, a report, a straightforward argument), but that doesn't really matter in the long run, I have nothing against him. If I were to do something like that I would feel diminished in all that is strongest and most personal about me, in my 'private', intimate autonomy. Because if literature is not pure art, it is nevertheless the voice of an individual, of a private man. It is a grandiose and a magnificent thing that a pen and a piece of paper should suffice for someone to write what he likes, in his own name, for his own sake, for his own satisfaction, without obeying any code, without any subjection or limitation. Of course, nobody knows better than I how illusory this independence is, yet it still brings us closest to our individual reality. And in a society which suppressed the liberty and independence of literature nobody would know what was going on inside the private individual.

So much, then, for my views as a writer. Personally, of course, I have some rather amateurish convictions. One man tends towards the right, the other towards the left. So I, too, have tendencies. I place myself at the extreme left. I am on the side of the proletariat and that is the only reason why I am against Communism. I say it frankly and as seriously as possible.

I am an atheist with no prejudices and, in addition to that, I am pro-Semitic. I am also an *avant-garde* writer, a 'destroyer' in a certain sense. So how could I be a diehard conservative? I lived for twenty-five years in penury and, as far as my personal interests are concerned, I could only gain by a social revolution. My literary colleagues in the socialist countries enjoy a far more privileged position than I do. There is nothing in my present position which ties me to the capitalist classes. In view of all this, I would have to be a monster to prefer exploitation to justice, just like that, as a matter of taste. That can only happen if, consciously or unconsciously, selfish interests come into play or if one remains trapped in the claws of atavism.

Ah yes! I am for the proletariat: that is to say that I am against it since I would like it to vanish from the face of the earth! But look . . . it is vanishing far more swiftly in the capitalist countries of the West. In the East, the mass of workers live as they have always lived and I can see no prospect of improvement in the near future. I am in no position to embark on a complicated economic dissertation. What I want is an end to be put to that disgrace called proletariat, so I am on the side of the system which puts an end to it best.

I am bound to the Communists by a common goal—I only disagree with them on the choice of methods. That is why I say I am extremely left-wing. And if we call anyone who wants to abolish class a Communist, then the most ardent conservative can be considered a Communist provided he frankly believes that a prudent conservative policy will serve this purpose better than a destructive and gruesome revolution.

This proves the relativity of the notion of the 'left'.

Furthermore, since Freud and Marx have revealed so many things, wouldn't it be useful to look behind that façade which we call the 'left'? I am grieved by the fact that the left all too often becomes a screen covering personal interests which are, we must admit, completely selfish and imperialistic. An ambitious politician, a writer eager to be heard, a team of journalists who realize that opposition raises the sales of their paper, a young man searching for an outlet for his natural exuberance . . . aren't all these people instinctively going to turn to the left? Socialism becomes an instrument in the hands of the liberalism which hides behind it. Liberalism as such doesn't frighten me, but mystification on too great a scale does. That's why I think that honest men who belong to the left should control the left in some way. The time has come to study the conditioning of consciousness not only among the capitalist sharks but also in the student who shouts insults at a meeting.

But it certainly won't be me who will perform this role. I am a declared enemy of all roles, and particularly of that of the committed writer. I am sorry, but I really can't be of any use there. I am too sure that in a very short time science and mechanization will blow the opposition between right and left from under our noses and will place before us some radically different problems.

Politics? My policy is to weaken forms—it matters little whether they are left- or right-wing.

France. Do I like living in France? Of course. How could I not? France is a 'closed' country. Form is constantly being worked and created, and, at the same time, nobody is as capable as the Frenchman of putting Form into doubt, both by joking and by being serious. So I don't dislike living in France at all. But, to tell the truth, I feel all the better in France since Paris is at the very heart of the crisis of Form which we are now going through. Consequently, all the ailments of Form appear there in a particularly obvious and aggravating way. Paris maddens me and nothing is healthier, especially for people of a certain age. Just as French artists and writers of yesterday and the day before yesterday seem to me incredibly stimulating, so, as far as I'm concerned, recent French literature might just as well not exist. This doesn't apply only to French literature, but the French occupy first place.

Sartre, that eminent Frenchman, seems to me a good illustration of what I call the crisis of Form in France . . . at least as far as the Cartesian tradition is concerned. When you read *Being and Nothingness* you have that feeling which only truly creative works give you. It is a book which aims at *you*, you personally, and keeps its eye on you . . . and I, I suddenly recognized myself in it, when I laid my hands on it, down there, in the Argentine. Take the 'being for itself' which descends straight from Descartes—is that not the most radical manner of setting the problem of Form? Subjectivity, nothingness and liberty, the free creation of value, doesn't all this imply distance from Form? And is it not incredible and marvellous that the existentialist tendency towards the concrete (in my case towards reality) should be tragically duplicated, fractionalized by this little word 'for', and saturated with distance, with nothingness? Consequently, it is outside ourselves that we must search for man. On the other hand isn't 'being for others' just as radical an assertion that we are the object of other people's Form, that we are deformed by Form? This is one of the reasons why Sartre appeared to me as the codifier of my own feelings. But in the subsequent pages of the book, I was in for a terrible disappointment! For, having led his man to so radical a freedom that it compromises all possibility of Form (in the sphere of the 'for itself' the being is nothing but the perpetual creation of the being) Sartre suddenly escapes from subjectivity and his thought takes a path which confines man in ever stricter rules, shuts him in an increasingly defined Form. Well, I felt a little like Husserl when confronted by Descartes' 'fatal deviation', at the moment when Cartesian philosophy takes a leap towards God and the world. Wasn't this the second time that this had happened to French Cartesianism? Terrified by its audacity, it betrayed itself.

To my mind Cartesianism contains both the possibility of Form and of distance from Form, the possibility either of a radical subjectivism or of the most arid objective rigour. These two tendencies define the living dialectic of the French mind. When Sartre lets himself be dragged into the system, the codification, the Form, when *Being and Nothingness* (not to mention his other works) is transformed into a sort of moral tract, this 'deviation' seems very indicative of the French crisis of Form. There is the logical Frenchman and the artistic Frenchman, the systematic Frenchman and the spontaneous Frenchman, the serious Frenchman and the smiling Frenchman, the Frenchman as a producer and the Frenchman as a consumer. Through science, Marxism and Marxicized existentialism, the dry, cerebral, speculative and anti-artistic (because anti-subjective) spirit of France was stimulated furiously, while French elasticity, the innocent malleability of Montaigne or Rimbaud, was stifled and obstructed.

France will remain alive as long as her need for Form is counterbalanced by an equal distrust of Form. At the moment something is being spoiled in the Frenchman's profound frivolity. Surrealism, the most violent protest of the French mind against the threats of Form, was corrupted by the intellect from the start. It was thirsting for logic, for intellectual, scientific, and philosophical justification. The invasion of art by science met with no serious resistance because the artist couldn't muster enough passion, enthusiasm, poetry, a sufficiently concrete reality or enough fun or frivolity. All the mechanisms of an increasingly mechanized culture which have led art to become increasingly artificial, the poet to become more of a 'poet', the painter more of a 'painter', the genius more of a 'genius', rose in value and such an overdone, elaborate language has imposed itself that today, in Paris, people no longer really know what they are saying. Beauty, too, is coming to an end. I sometimes wonder why I don't like Proust. It is that atmosphere of tail coats and dressing gowns which repels me so much. Never does he leave his milieu, even for a second. This martyr knew death and suffering and the terrible traps of existence, but, as far as beauty and charm were concerned, he could never liberate himself. He had enough energy to turn Montesquieu into a Charlus, but in the aesthetic sphere he remained Montesquieu's vassal until the end. His depth, his acuteness, his analyses, yes, they all work quite well. But his ecstasy, his charm, his seduction has the tang of a beauty parlour and a boudoir, they have something sickly and fashionable about them: they are 'dainty'.

I have always regarded French beauty as fragile and hazardous in a way, because it stems more from civilization than from nature. Versailles undoubtedly has a form of beauty, but it is very suspect. It is almost ridiculous and ugly for the simple reason that it is artificial and refined. So the fate of French beauty depends on this: lightness must learn how to face up to those artificial and mannered products of a higher civilization and how to surpass them by mobilizing the most pedestrian and current elements of life. In this respect it is indicative that the only form of beauty truly admired by Proust, the beauty of a young boy, never actually penetrates the pages of his work, directly or indirectly. This, the most important aspect of beauty, is passed over in silence: it has no place in his style. By the light of Sartre and Proust, we see how France moves further and further away in its thought and its art from its cool and refreshing sources. And the Frenchman who, but recently, was reputed for his desire to please, now does all he can to displease—in literature and art at least. That is how the most stimulating culture in history is becoming increasingly repulsive.

Will the Frenchman still manage to establish contact with other Frenchmen? Or will he be content with a more abstract relationship, with the products of his own culture and that of others? You see: their novels are not written for the reader but for the critic. Their art is at the service of theory and their morals, their efforts to liberate themselves, to recover spontaneity and liberty, are premeditated and subordinated to the rules.

Surrealism was not the last attempt to rebel against this increasing rigidity. Even today there is no lack of rebels who struggle feverishly, like fish out of water. Their watchwords are 'direct communication', 'liberty', 'creation'. But what is the nature of these rebellions? What characterizes them all without exception is that they are spasmodic, convulsive, brutal and cold. They do not lead to any release but contribute, rather, to an increase of the spasm, the convulsion, the tension.

Lack of air. Everything is intensified, nothing relaxes. That fascinates me in France today. That stifling quality. That threat. That's exciting.

Structuralism. Yes, in a way I am a structuralist just as I am an existentialist. I am bound to structuralism by my approach to Form. Of course, the human personality, which I believe is created 'between men', in the human context which denies it, is part of a system of dependencies by no means dissimilar to a 'structure'. In what I wrote before the war, you will find expressions which have now been incorporated by the structuralists. Take the passage in *Ferdydurke* to which I have already referred where I suggested replacing 'I believe this, I feel that, I am this, I stand for that' by 'In me there is a belief, a feeling, a thought, I am the vehicle for such-and-such an action, production, or whatever it may be . . . '

Or, even in *The Marriage,* Henry's 'It is not we who say the words, it is the words which say us.' Pure coincidence? No. Their world is almost my world. Almost. Because it is also the opposite.

I wage an eternal war against science. Structuralism originates in ethnology, linguistics, mathematics and, in its widest sense, as in Foucault, it is epistemology. My structuralism, on the other hand, is artistic, it comes from the street and from everyday reality, it is practical. And because it is practical it is seasoned with anguish and passion. The structuralists uncover Form coldly, while I do so warmly: I am scared of it! And I play with it!

Though this might be interpreted as a desire to blow my own trumpet in their cerebral orchestra I must say quite frankly that the fact that none of these great intellects should have paid any attention to my work seems somewhat unfortunate. My literature is not derived from structuralism (like most things nowadays): it was born independently and it arrived at conclusions similar to those of the structuralists. But I approached things in a different state of mind, on a different level, after different experiences. Yet my reality is authentic, and scientists should not be indifferent to the fact that an artist travels in the same direction as they, like a passenger on another train, on a parallel line.

But what separates us is more important than what we have in common. I, a private and concrete individual, hate structures, and if I reveal Form in my way, it is in order to defend myself.

Modesty and absence of modesty. I would like to apologize to my reader for my incapacity to convey, even approximately, the greatness, the power, the majesty, the horror of my life. Of course my life, like every man's life, is a hundred times more gigantic. So please excuse an excess of *modesty* which has led to too modest results.

I must also apologize for my *absence of modesty.* For I have served up something like a *romanticized autobiography*, embellishing and dramatizing the bleakness of my existence. I did this so as not to tire my reader. These pages are intended for a wide readership. I would like them to be accessible and, as far as possible, to be colourful.

If someone told me that I was *acting at being a genius* (I don't think that will happen, but one never knows) I would say that I don't reply to such idiotic accusations.

The truth. I don't think I have moved too far from the truth.

I know nothing is more dangerous than to guide people through one's own work. Art is always *something more* and it is precisely in that that it escapes from the interpretation which approaches it most closely. I have abbreviated it, impoverished it . . . but an author whose work has been as badly read as mine does not have much to lose. This little book could be a useful guide, but one shouldn't expect too much from it. Its main defect is to linger too much on form and not to introduce the reader sufficiently to another of my preoccupations: immaturity.

I shall even admit that throughout these pages I retained the impression that my work was elsewhere. I mean: if my work had to serve this vision of man and the world exclusively it should have been written rather differently. Of course, this vision is contained in it, but that was not why I wrote it. Writing, for me, is primarily a game. It has no plan and no aim. That is why I cannot really extract an ideological system from it. I must again emphasize that it is an *a posteriori* system.

A summing-up: How many pages have I written in my life? About three thousand. Why, if they're all about myself? I wrote this book in order to link my work with my life. Well, did my work help me to solve my problems, my personal difficulties?

I am almost ashamed of myself. Where have my assaults on Form got me? To Form. I broke it so much and so often that I became the writer whose subject is Form. That is my form and my definition. And today I, a living individual, am the servant of that official Gombrowicz whom I built with my own hands. I can only add to him. My former impulses, my gaffes, my dissonances, all this trying immaturity . . . where has all that gone? In my old age, life has become easier for me. I sail confidently between my contradictions and people listen to what I have to say. Yes, yes, I've dug my hole, I've played my part. I am a servant. Whose? Gombrowicz's.

Will my former revolt sow a seed in someone else's youthful and triumphant imagination? I don't know. But how about me? Will I ever again be able to rebel against him, against that other Gombrowicz? I'm not at all sure. I've contemplated various tricks which would have enabled me to escape from this tyranny, but age and ill-health have removed my means. To get rid of that other Gombrowicz, to compromise him, destroy him, would certainly be vivifying . . . but nothing is more arduous than to fight against one's own shell.

To return to the time before the beginning, to seek refuge in my initial immaturity. (This Immaturity is still more important to me than Form, but I haven't said too much about it in this book because it isn't easy to discuss it and I would rather people looked for it in the live matter of my artistic work.)

But to rebel? How? Me? A servant?

SELECTED DALKEY ARCHIVE PAPERBACKS

FOR A FULL LIST OF PUBLICATIONS, VISIT:

www.dalkeyarchive.com

SELECTED DALKEY ARCHIVE PAPERBACKS

FOR A FULL LIST OF PUBLICATIONS, VISIT:

www.dalkeyarchive.com